VIA NEGATIVA

Via Negativa

❧

Daniel Hornsby

ALFRED A. KNOPF   NEW YORK   2020

THIS IS A BORZOI BOOK PUBLISHED BY ALFRED A. KNOPF

www.aaknopf.com

Library of Congress Cataloging-in-Publication Data
Names: Hornsby, Daniel, author.
Title: Via negativa / Daniel Hornsby.
Description: New York : Alfred A. Knopf, 2020. |
Identifiers: LCCN 2019049923 (print) | LCCN 2019049924
    (ebook) | ISBN 9780525658474 (hardcover) |
    ISBN 9780525658481 (ebook)
Subjects: LCSH: Priests—Fiction. | Life change events—Fiction. |
    Retribution—Fiction. | Religious fiction. | GSAFD: Humorous
    fiction.
Classification: LCC PS3608.O7673 V53 2020 (print) |
    LCC PS3608.O7673 (ebook) | DDC 813/.6—dc23
LC record available at https://lccn.loc.gov/2019049923
LC ebook record available at https://lccn.loc.gov/2019049924

Portions of this work originally appeared in slightly different
form as "The Desert Fathers (Three Episodes from the Diary of a
Retired Priest)" in *Joyland* on January 1, 2019.

Jacket illustration and design by Tyler Comrie

Manufactured in Canada
First Edition

FOR MY MOTHER AND FATHER

VIA NEGATIVA

1

Somebody hit a coyote and I pulled over to the shoulder to take a look at it.

I'd watched it bounce off a minivan twenty yards ahead of me. A gold smudge. At first I thought it might have been a paper bag tossed out the window, or maybe an old T-shirt, until I saw its big yellow eyes and tail flopping around as it skittered onto the gravel, rolling like a stuntman on fire.

By the time I walked up to it on the shoulder, it was lying on its side, taking quick, shallow breaths and staring up past my head. One of its legs looked like it had an extra joint.

I reached out to touch it, and it didn't bite. I ran my finger along its hind leg, and it didn't move.

With a spare blanket from the trunk, I wrapped him up (I could now see he was male, for whatever that's worth), then stuck him in the back seat, next to the bucket, the books, and my duffel bag.

I grabbed two of the books and shoved the rest into the footwell so they wouldn't shift onto him. I set the coyote's head on the selected writings of Origen of Alexandria and wedged my collection of the Venerable Bede's homilies between the seat belt and the blanket to brace the animal's ribs and diffuse the pressure of the strap when I buckled him in. He was panting hard, so I poured some water into his mouth and, after I'd made sure his tongue had drawn it in, poured a little more on the blanket for him to suck on if he got thirsty soon. Before I drove off, I stuck half a Niravam in his mouth and heard it fizzle on his tongue.

Origen, that spiritual genius of the second and third centuries, says we can go up or down from age to age. Someone could be a monk, and then, after a snobby life of chastity and starvation, come back as an angel. Or you could go backward—you might come to as an animal (a pigeon, a rat, a coyote), and then drop to demon, or go down to whatever is below that. The idea behind this being that at the beginning of time we were all made of fire and turned toward God in constant, sizzling contemplation, burning up His divine fumes. Most minds (with the sole exception of Jesus, he says) turned from Him, became distracted, and cooled, and from then on we were stuck with our husky bodies. Now we can go up or down. But eventually even those at the bottom will climb their way back up to God, when time calls it quits.

I haven't read Origen in a while, admittedly, but I'm pretty sure that's the gist of his cosmic scheme. Which he would say is somewhat metaphorical anyhow.

Thanks to a couple first-millennium controversies

among the monasteries of Lower Egypt, Origen was never canonized. There are pictures of him standing at the pulpit, preaching to a congregation of saints (Augustine, Ambrose), a haloed crowd in which he's the only one with no light shooting out of his head.

Somewhere in Illinois, I changed the blanket. The coyote had pissed and shit in it. A good sign, I figured, but the car was beginning to smell. He left a foamy stripe of puke on Origen, and some of it smeared onto Bede.

I wrapped him in one of my towels at a rest stop. He was as light as a throw pillow. He didn't move at all.

The back leg looked pretty bad, bent slightly the wrong way. When I touched it, he jerked out of his daze and snapped his jaws. I'd need to set the bone.

A woman stepped out of the van parked next to me.

"Got yourself a little buddy there, Father?"

She walked over, and before I could stop her she stroked his nose.

"Doesn't like to travel. I gave him one of those pills. He's a little out of it."

"I can tell. Well, I hope he gets there safe. You too. God bless."

I buckled him back in and threw the blanket into the trash.

Bede joined the monastery of Monkwearmouth when he was seven. As an oblate. A *puer oblatus*. Literally, a "child offered," part of a practice of dedicating prepubescent boys to monastic life. It probably wasn't the best for child development, but the monks who did this moved through scripture like fish in water, my theology professor used to say.

I went to the minor seminary at fourteen. St. John Bosco's. This was in Indiana, in the sixties, but there are still a few places like that. It's the closest thing to being an oblate you can get in recent memory. There were a lot of oblates in the Middle Ages—it simplified inheritance to send off a second-born son (or ninth-born, in my case) to a monastery before he reached puberty. Many of the best medieval scholars were oblates. William of Ockham was an oblate. So was St. Boniface, I think.

I roomed with three other boys, and we were far from little Bedes or Ockhams. We found the room where the older priests kept their whiskey, gin, and cartons of cigarettes and broke into it all the time. Sometimes we'd hitchhike into Indianapolis and try to meet girls. More than once a couple of us brought some back to the seminary and made out in the grounds' charitable shadows. The priests didn't object to this as much as you might think. The boys were trying to get one last look at what they'd be giving up, should they graduate to the major seminary and go through with ordination. I don't know what the girls were trying to get. The seminary was not a romantic place. Everywhere you looked, a saint or an angel was there watching you—staring up and to the side, the way they always do.

Last night, a couple hours after I picked up the coyote, I stopped at a campground off the highway. I parked the car near a tree inscribed with the message "JB WAS HERE FUUCK RON!" I almost stepped on a Kentucky Fried Chicken bucket. Some animal had torn it apart. The colonel's face stared back at me, mutilated and sinister, like a zombie's.

I unloaded my supplies from the Camry. They'd given me two weeks to move out of the rectory, and in that time I ran a number of tests. I took a bucket and one of those circular cushions they make you wear when you break your tailbone, and with these I'd made a kind of chamber pot. I soldered together a foldable grill. I have a master's in art, and I've always been pretty good at making things. Over the years, I kept picking up new crafts. I've worked with pewter, clay, wood, PVC pipe, and (in one disastrous project) human hair. So it was fun for me to put these things together.

Something in my knee popped when I reached in to

grab my tent. It was so loud even the coyote turned his head to see what was going on. But it didn't hurt too bad. I'd be all right as long as I didn't fully extend my leg.

Despite his curiosity about my knee, the coyote was still pretty dazed. I put on a pair of leather driving gloves and bound him up in the towel, leaving his broken leg sticking out like a kettle's spout. I buckled him back in so he couldn't turn and bite me. And then I took some plaster gauze from my first aid kit and started wrapping the broken leg with it. The coyote didn't like this and started wriggling, but then he passed out—because of the pain, I think. With him lying still, I managed to get the leg set pretty straight, and used up most of the gauze, because it seemed likely he'd chew through it if there wasn't enough. I drizzled water on the wraps so they would hold and then turned up the air so the plaster would set faster. Once he came to, I gave him the other half of the pill.

When I was done, he looked like one of those mummified cats you see pictures of in *National Geographic*.

With the coyote bundled up, I pitched my tent. Lying there in the dark, I thought I heard something or someone moving through the trees about fifty yards away. I pulled out my flashlight and shined it into the brush, but there wasn't anything. If you're alone long enough, your mind begins to populate the world. I think that's why the Desert Fathers—St. Antony, Arsenius—were always battling demons. I'm not saying those demons weren't real; I just think you have to be alone for a long time if your brain is going to be able to see anything special.

I grabbed one of the books from the car and tried to read it by flashlight. After mindlessly skimming a few pages, I felt something sticky on the spine. Some of the coyote's bile had caked onto it. I wiped it off on the side of the tent.

I fell asleep about an hour after that.

2

There are guitar-playing priests, and there are pre–Vatican II priests, and there are Eisenhower priests. There are pedophile priests and there are communist priests. There are pot-smoking priests (subcategory of guitar-playing priests) and alcoholic priests (functioning, tragic, or, that fine balance, Irish). There are gun-owning priests, golfing priests, and tennis-playing priests. There are gay priests and there are priests that are much too straight. There are poetry-reading priests and there are Merton-esque meditating priests, categories I might fall under. There are young priests—an increasingly conservative lot, nostalgic for the pre–Vatican II days they've never had to live through—and there are retired priests, a designation that now applies to me. In fact, I might be considered in the category of "retired-retired priest," given my current peripatetic status. Not simply a priest without a parish, but a priest without a rectory, an address, or a home.

But all priests are supposed to be without homes. I signed up for it.

I've been living out of the car for about a month now, and I think I could go on like this forever. At first, hygiene was a worry. But I've found the showers at truck stops wholly satisfactory, and I clean out the bucket with dish soap every chance I get, and there have been no problems so far. Loneliness was another concern, but I was lonelier in the rectories, surrounded by dying priests mumbling guesses along to *The Price Is Right.* Out here, I have the opportunity to run into people all the time. If I wanted to, I could visit old parishioners who moved away, or the odd acquaintance from retreats, and if my back starts hurting and I want a warm meal and a shower, I can always stay at a local parish for a night and get back in the car in the morning.

I've tried to make the car into a mobile monk's cell. Of course, I really can't compare myself to those great mothers and fathers of the desert, but I'm trying to see myself as their disciple, a fellow anchorite trying to rely more and more on God in all aspects of my life. Or, to put it another way, I'm a pilgrim, on my way to some holy place.

But even that is too lofty. I am a retired priest living in his car. I am a retired-retired priest, kicked out of his rectory and living in his car with a coyote and a bucket he shits in.

※

My parish in Muncie was named after one of those Desert Fathers. Antony the Great. Antony of the Desert.

Antony the Anchorite. Patron of gravediggers and skin disease. The first to wander off into the desert to do battle with hideous demons and wild beasts, to live in caves, eating almost nothing and praying all day long.

When I think back to my years at St. Antony's (which I now have plenty of time to do, driving around—it's almost all I do), two very strange ceremonies stand out to me, as theological puzzles of sorts.

The first is perhaps the more straightforward, my role having been very minor. Sometime during my first five years as pastor, I walked into my rectory office and found two strange men sitting there, waiting to speak with me. One wore a leather jacket and several gold rings. The other had a tattoo on his neck, a crescent moon a few inches below his ear. His hair was short. His head looked like a fist covered in sandpaper. We sat there in my office, and the one with the tattoo explained that his father had been king of the Gypsies in Indiana, and that he'd just passed away. I gave him my condolences, and he went on to explain that it was custom for his people to hold a wake, one that lasted at least three days, and that for his father it was no different. Except it was different, because his father had been king, so the sheer number of people expected to pay homage would be significant. He'd approached two other priests but had been turned away. So, they asked, could they use my church?

I agreed to do it on the spot. Wasn't Christ a king who'd been denied shelter? Wasn't it our responsibility to take care of those with nowhere else to go? I arranged to cancel Saturday Mass so they could stay from Thursday through Saturday. I called the head of maintenance and briefed him on the wake. I felt good about it. But it turns out I'd taken on more than I knew. For one thing, I soon learned, it was part of the tradition for the Roma in those parts to eat and drink a great deal in the presence of the body, the belief being that anything consumed near the casket would sustain the king in the afterlife. I couldn't let people get drunk and party in the sanctuary space, so I booked the feast in the parish hall, which was technically under the same roof as the sanctuary where the king would lie. More significantly, it was the number of people staying in the hall that presented the greatest problem. At one point we had almost two hundred mourners on the grounds, drinking cans of beer from a kiddie pool, dancing on the linoleum, and smoking outside the building, by a long line of black motorcycles and a silver horse-trailer. Later, the heir apparent was involved in a fight in the parking lot—some issue of succession now resolved, he assured me afterward. But despite a few phone calls from concerned parishioners (the Saturday crowd, I suspect; people who regularly attend Saturday evening Mass are the most dull and mechanical Catholics and should technically be considered Presbyterian), I saw no issue at the time, and certainly did not expect it to become the ordeal it turned into.

I dipped down there a few times over the course of the wake, to show my support. I drank wine and beer, watched the families dance and the kids chase each other around. The community felt real, more than an empty ritual. I reassured myself that I'd done the right thing.

On the first night, the prince pulled me aside and poured me some wine in a plastic cup. He had a cut on his cheek the same color as the wine. There was a fleck of dried blood dangling off the moon under his ear.

"I hated that old man," he said. "I'm going to miss the shit out of him."

He opened a bag of frozen peas and spooned some into his mouth. One rolled across the cafeteria table. It was still frosted and looked like a cold green planet on the edge of a tiny solar system.

"My dad hated peas, so I thought I'd stick it to him a little. Have some."

I chipped off two or three peas and ate them. They were crunchy and sweet, and their skins stuck to my teeth.

A very large man fell into the kiddie pool filled with cans of beer, sending a tide of icy water and Coors Lights onto the tile.

"Father, you good? You drunk yet? Your cheeks look a little red."

I was fine, I said, and told him to tell me more about the king.

"Dad was tough. He didn't take any shit. When I was younger I thought he was a tyrant, that he was a complete dick. But now I think he was fair. He didn't want to show me any special treatment, but I also think it made him kind of cold or something. I left the family and lived in Vegas for a couple years, and when that didn't work out, he took me back like I'd never been gone. Which was why I had to take care of that guy in the parking lot. Sorry again for that."

"It seems like a pretty interesting life. What made you leave?"

"There's a lot of responsibility. You probably have a kind of image in your head of hippie Gypsies, like from some Grateful Dead song or something, who are always Django Reinhardt–ing around with guitars and earrings. But, growing up, it was the opposite of freedom. There was a lot of pressure on me, to lead a community and reflect well on him, to be good and right all of the time. You probably know what that can be like."

"Maybe, yeah."

"How do you handle the responsibility and everything?"

I knew I should mutter a few homiletic lines, satisfy him with a little useless aphorism, but I couldn't muster it right then.

"It's hard. I don't know if I was made to lead people. I think I should have become a monk."

I was joking, but it occurred to me that I'd spoken the truth. I wasn't a very good pastor, or parish priest, for that matter. I was stubborn and prone to prickly megrims. I didn't mind the theater of the Mass, but other public appearances, pretty much any gathering of two or more over which I was expected to hold court, filled me with dread beforehand and left me feeling hollow. As my coming reckoning with the bishop would prove, I would've done much better in some remote monastery on a chalky Italian cliff, or Thomas Merton's quiet patch of rural Kentucky. Or some other century.

Maybe, I thought as I talked to the prince, I'd misheard my calling, or, worse: God had dialed the wrong number.

The prince squeezed the bag of peas with both hands, breaking the frozen mass into chunks through the plastic.

"He wasn't exactly touchy-feely, but, looking back, I know that piece of shit loved me."

He ate another spoonful of peas, sealed off the bag, and then held the cold package against the cuts on his face.

On the third day, the last day of the wake, he pulled me aside again.

"We have to do the blessing," he said, and we walked up the stairs to the sanctuary.

"You guys ready?" the prince shouted into the dark of the nave.

Two teenage boys with electric guitars appeared. Both had blond hair that reached their waists and covered their faces in frizzy veils. They suited the courtly air. They looked like medieval maidens, two sisters who wove tapestries and played their golden harps in some dim castle.

"All right. Father's gonna say a prayer, and then you guys bust out a song. Sound good?"

The prince flipped open the lid of the casket. Inside lay the small and shriveled king, with his tattooed hands clutching a bundle of gold rosaries and his long gray hair pulled behind his ears. These locks, along with the solemn expression on his face, truly did give him a look of nobility. It was easy to imagine him as some dead Merovingian known for his wisdom and valor.

I said a blessing, invoking St. Sarah, the patron of the Roma. The kids tuned their guitars and started into a version of "All Along the Watchtower." The prince sat there in the pew and stared at the body of his father, the king.

That week, I received a phone call from the bishop. Some of my parishioners were concerned, he said, and if in the future I wanted to offer the space for any unusual purposes, I was to contact him first. Thus began our long period of tension, a tug-of-war that would last nearly three decades and cause me no small amount of worry. It was part of why I'm here, now, sitting in my car somewhere in Illinois. At the time I wondered if I'd done the wrong thing, but I've since thought my impulse to have been correct.

Years later, however, I'm afraid the effect of the bishop's reprimands caused me to make the wrong decision, one I regret.

3

This morning, I gave the coyote a couple hours to recover without being bumped around the back seat. I got to driving around nine.

I put in a Lorde CD once I got on the highway. A girl in one of the youth groups gave it to me when I told her what kind of music I liked. It's a couple years old, but I still enjoy it. My favorite singer, though, is Prince. I have five or six of his CDs crammed in the cubby behind the cup holders, along with a few other odds and ends: pens and pencils, a cigarette lighter, an old letter in a green envelope from a friend in Colorado. There is a real mystical theology to Prince, and I'm not being cheeky.

For breakfast I stopped at a Cracker Barrel in Effingham, Illinois. To my right sat a pack of men in camouflage, wolfing down biscuits and gray breakfast sausages. I sat at a table by myself, under a pair of snowshoes and a hatchet nailed to the wall.

Before I ordered, I went to the bathroom to wash my hands and make sure there wasn't anything stuck in my beard. I've been working on growing a beard for a while now. I thought it might help me get into character. I'd always wanted to grow one when I was a pastor, but, owing to a barren stripe on my cheek, I could never quite get there without looking ridiculous for a couple patchy weeks. Now I've plowed through this phase, with enough hair to fluff over the bald spot. I'm about halfway between a Francis and a Peter. Nothing quite Old Testament yet, still several months from an Antony. Aside from a teal smudge of toothpaste, I looked okay.

I pulled out my road atlas and spread it out on the table. I wasn't in any rush. I was in the opposite of a rush. Eventually, I would get to Seattle to see my friends Clara and Brian, but I had a lot more time to get there than I needed.

I'd marked Clara and Brian's house with a Dole sticker from a banana I picked up when I left Indiana. I traced my route with the tines of my fork, first to a suburb outside of Denver to see my friend Paul, then on to Seattle, all the way up to the shimmering halo in the middle of the Dole "o." There was still a cloud of gluey residue over eastern Montana. I rubbed it off with my thumb and flicked the last white pellets off the table.

Clara and Brian had gone to my church. Clara had been an art professor at (the unfortunately named) Ball State University; Brian did something with computers. They weren't married when I met them. For years Clara and I had worked together on art projects for the worship space: an avant-garde Advent wreath, abstract (and very unpopular) renderings of the stations of the cross, special Jubilee doors for the Year 2000. We went hiking together, to museums together. She grew up in Jalisco, Mexico, and had an artistic, even witchy take on Catholicism that I found refreshing among the bland near-Protestantism of Midwestern Catholics. She was the one who encouraged me to get my master's, and then served as my adviser when I did. Later on, I was her spiritual adviser and led her through the exercises of St. Ignatius.

When she married Brian, I married them. That sounds wrong. But maybe it's not entirely untrue. I was with them all the time. I ate dinner with them twice a week, one night at their place, another in the rectory. They brought me along on their vacations—first to Los Angeles to see a Louise Bourgeois retrospective, and, later, on a trip to Puebla, Mexico, where we visited a sixteenth-century convent she'd been researching. I love my family, but even though I was one of nine children, I was a loner from early on. Brian and Clara were like my new family, probably beyond what is appropriate, given my vocation. I loved them too much, and the congregation knew it. One day, one of my parishioners, a lector, made a joke about how they were my favorites, and it bothered me. I had crossed a line. I'd clearly shown favoritism. After this (and I'm not sure it was a completely conscious effort), I began to spend less and less time with the two of them. And then they moved away. Brian received an offer for a better job in Seattle, so much better that Clara would be able to work on her art full-time. They finally got out of Indiana, like they always wanted to.

They tried to get me to move out to Seattle with them once I retired, five years ago, but I didn't. I don't know why I didn't. I just went where the bishop sent me, and went somewhere else after that, and now I've been kicked out of my rectory and I'm living in my car and driving to visit them.

I've occasionally been grateful not to have been a fisherman in Galilee 2,000-plus years ago. I worry I would have been asked to follow and wouldn't have been able to. I'm afraid I would've just kept on fishing.

But I am probably only thinking about fishing because of a strange story one of the waiters told me.

"So you're a priest?" my waitress asked after she took my order and saw my collar.

I told her I was.

"Priests creep me out," she said. "No offense. My older brother told me that priests did spells and performed sacrifices on cats and babies, and I still kind of think that, even though I know it's not actually true. I still think you could do a spell right now. If you levitated that knife or spoon, I would not be surprised at all. Just full-on Dumbledored it." She flicked a glob of gravy off her sleeve. "My dad was Catholic. So I am, pretty much biologically. We never really went to church, though. I don't actually believe in churches. But I'm still not an atheist, because I think there are a lot of things that can't be fully explained. Things that defy scientific explanation. Shadowy-ish things. I know people who've seen them."

"Like what?"

"Very weird kinds of things."

Another waiter, who'd been resetting the table beside mine, interjected.

"I knew this guy who could eat glass. He'd just break off a chunk and eat it like a piece of peanut brittle. I watched him chomp down a beer bottle in under fifteen minutes—we timed him. He said he liked the mouthfeel. Made his teeth wear down, so he had to stop."

"Not like that," my waitress said, and he shrugged and walked off to one of his tables.

"Like what?" I asked again.

I hadn't talked to anyone, besides just buying gas or food, in three days, so I was eager for the conversation.

"Here." I reached into my wallet and pulled out two fives. "I'll add ten dollars to the tip."

I was trying hard not to be creepy. Which, I know, can really only make you creepier.

"Creepy" usually means one of two things, and I knew she probably meant both. There was Halloween creepy, and there was pervert creepy. She had tried to put her emphasis on the spooky connotation, but of course that was only to paste over the pedophilia. And the antidote? I cupped my hands around my coffee mug. I tried not to smile too much (as to seem too eager to talk), but still smiled occasionally, so I wouldn't seem like a humorless psychopath.

She checked on another table. I thought that I'd failed, that I'd actually creeped her out by bribing her to report her miracles, but then she came back to bring me more coffee.

"Okay," she said. "So my mom says she sees these weird orbs. For a long time, every night in her room she would see these orbs of light flying around. Sometimes just racing right past her and disappearing. They'd come in blue at times, she says, but other times she said they were white or yellowy. She says she knew they were good, in a gut way—she knew they represented goodness, on some level. When she was a girl, she asked God to help her see angels, and she's not sure if they are that or not. My dad thinks they are souls going back to God. He insists angels have wings, but I think that is just a symbol, the way we say God has hands. Or eyes. He can't see them, anyway. Nowadays it's not even every night she sees them, though. She says she'd grown fond of the little guys. She misses them."

She topped off my coffee again.

"Do you think it was real?" she asked.

This is just the kind of thing I love. I told her about

the summer I tried to make myself see visions in the dome I'd built on the parish grounds. I had to backtrack some, to tell her about the construction of the geodesic dome itself, another one of my projects.

Before I moved to the last rectory, they put me in a parish in Crawfordsville. The pastor took pretty good care of me—I think I was too lefty or artsy for his taste, friendship-wise, but he let me work on my projects and left me alone. At that time, owing to a biography of Michelangelo I'd picked up at a garage sale, I was really into domes. With a design I found in the library, I built a large geodesic dome on the grounds—just past the tree line, so no one would have to see it from the rectory. It took me two months. And when I was done I built another one, a little-sister dome off to the side, connected to the first by a short hallway. They really are wonders of design. Easy to build, structurally sound, acoustically interesting, and naturally well insulated. I put a workshop in one and used the other as a retreat space, where I could get away from the other retired priests and their mind-numbing reruns, gossip, crossword puzzles, and daytime talk shows. I did my metalwork in the dome, read, meditated. Some nights I'd fall asleep there and wake up to the sounds of birds and squirrels scuttling across the tiles.

I decided I'd try an experiment out there. I'd read a magazine article about these trial runs to cure people's lazy eyes by keeping them in complete darkness for a whole week. After a few days, the subjects began to experience visual hallucinations—flashing lights and mysterious shapes surfacing from the dark. I wanted very badly to know what that was like. So I covered the big dome with a couple black tarps and plugged the crack under the door with a towel. I told the secretary at the rectory I was on a retreat (not really a lie), and I packed water and dry-good provisions requiring no stove or fire. I brought in my old guitar and labeled a couple audio-book CDs with foam stickers. I stayed in there for four days, spending most of this time bumping into things and trying not to bump into things. On the third day, while I sat trying to change a guitar string in total darkness, I thought I saw a blue spark in the middle of the room. Static, maybe. But it didn't go away. It floated up, and then I saw a blue hexagon, hovering about a yard over my head. I reached out to touch it, but it was too far, or it moved. It began to spin, and then blurred into a circle. The blue was the color of a butterfly wing. The circle shrank into nothing and popped out of existence. I waited for one more day in case I'd see something else, but nothing showed up after that.

When I came out, my legs were covered in maroon-and-indigo bruises, weird galaxies up and down my shins. And then, one day, I felt I should stop making stuff out there. I looked around my studio and asked myself if my art had ever fed anyone. No, it hadn't. Had it ever clothed anyone? No (with the exception of a coat I'd made for my nephew, which was more of a craft project). Did it ever comfort the sick or the imprisoned? Probably not. I gave away my tools and equipment to a stoner college kid I met at the art-supply store. I thought about dismantling the domes, too, but I couldn't bring myself to do it. They might still be there, for all I know, but my guess is, someone's taken them apart.

As I went on and on about the domes, my waitress swirled around the coffee into a black whirlpool, and her eyes kept moving back and forth from her other tables to the money on mine. I could see that I'd been talking too much, that my enthusiasm had overwhelmed her. I was a weird old man monologuing his dull dreams. I wrapped up my story as quickly as I could.

"I'm sorry, I'm rambling."

I slid her the two fives and immediately felt that this, rather than subtracting from my creepiness, only added to it. She left the bills there, the twin Lincolns inspecting the withered slug of a straw wrapper.

The other waiter, the one with the friend who ate glass, had been listening in by the drink station and now walked over.

"My brother just had a miracle happen to him a

few years ago. I don't know if it's truly a miracle. Maybe just supernatural?" He looked at me for confirmation, which I didn't feel I could offer. "I didn't see it, but he swears it's true," the waiter continued. "He was headed down to Port Aransas to do some fishing. My brother is a trucker, and he was between jobs, and instead of driving himself, he decided he was going to hitchhike. He had it all worked out, and brought his tackle and everything with him, as well as a knife in case things got hairy. Or thorny. He didn't need it, though, because he found someone headed pretty much the same place in one go. To Galveston. Or Port Arthur. But the thing was, the guy only had this one Carrie Underworld CD, and whenever my brother asked to change it, his driver was silent. So he listened to Carrie Underworld for hours on end."

My waitress: "Under*wood*. You keep saying it 'Under*world*.'"

"Really? I actually really like her, so that's weird. Are you sure?"

"Yeah."

"Huh." He pressed on. "So it's the same ten or eleven Carrie Under*wood* songs over and over again. Like, for five or six hours. He's hearing her in his sleep. He stuffs pieces of Kleenex in his ears, but that only muffles some of her, and by that point he knows the songs so well his brain can fill in the rest anyway. He's going crazy. But the guy was going to the same place he was, so what could he do?

"He did finally get to Port Aransas. It was late at night, but he couldn't sleep, because, every time he tries, he hears Carrie Underwood trying to sing into his dreams. So he goes right out to the public beach out there and sets up his pole and casts his line into the water and drinks some beer. You ever been to the Gulf?"

I told him I had a brother who used to live in Miami.

"So you know how funky that water can be. The character of it. It was late at night, and no one else was out there. It was all misty. He sat for a while and made his way through his first six-pack. He was just going to call it a night and go in when something tugged on the line. He fought with it for a while. He pulled with all his might, and he is a big guy, like me. Whatever it was, it was huge. A nurse shark, he thought, which would have been awesome. So he fights harder. It's like a battle.

"Then, after a long while, he sees it surface: this blonde girl sticking her head out of the water. It was Carrie Underwood herself. The same locks of golden hair from the CD case, the same skin, just about the same golden color as the hair. Except she was covered in eyes. She had eyes all over her face, eyes up and down her neck, eyes spotting her arms, shoulders, and clavicle, which was all he could see of her. And then she opened her mouth and sang."

The waiter closed his eyes and sang. His face filled up with blood, and the men in camouflage started staring at him.

Jesus, take the wheel
Take it from my hands . . .

"When she was done singing, her dozens of eyes looked him right in the eye and at that very moment he knew he'd have a job waiting for him when he got back to Illinois. And, sure enough, he did. His old company hired him back first thing. He's been back with them for four years now."

The waiter looked at us both with his eyes wide, nodded his head a few times to affirm what he believed to be our awed silence, and then blinked slowly, as if taking it all in for the first time himself.

"Fake," my waitress said, picking up the fives. "He just wants that miracle money."

I gave him a five, too. I would have to get better with my money, but I told myself I'd start tomorrow. I put my sausages into a doggy bag, to feed to the coyote.

He seemed to be coming out of it. I stuck another Niravam into the breakfast sausage, and the coyote chomped it down. He was still hungry, so I bought a tin of Spam at a gas station and scooped some into his mouth with a white plastic spoon. He ate it enthusiastically, licking the roof of his mouth the way a dog does when you feed it peanut butter. His eyes were big and yellow, and it was hard to look into them without being a little bit afraid.

Francis made a man-eating wolf repent. The Desert Fathers were known to heal the occasional hyena. I could never pull off thaumaturgical stunts like that, but I might be able to fix him the old-fashioned way.

Once he was drowsy, I changed the blanket again and tossed the gross old one into the trash.

Just a few miles down 70, I drove past a giant cross, maybe twenty stories high. It was made of white aluminum siding, a thousand garage doors fused together. It looked as if it'd been made to crucify Paul Bunyan. Some Protestant bullshit.

With the cross shrinking behind me, I screwed up my eyes, trying to picture the orbs my waitress's mother saw rising up from the cornfields. For the last couple

days, the same two or three sour thoughts had been circling my head, like cockroaches that spin around the
toilet bowl but refuse to flush down. I could have used
a vision.

The dome wasn't the first time I've tried to give
myself a mystical experience. I've spent a lot of time
experimenting, tweaking my methods, trying to glimpse
some weird and slippery thing. You may think that setting out to see these kinds of things is too artificial or
contrived, and because of this, whatever it is I may find
can't be genuine.

But that's wrong-minded. Most mystics and
prophets—even Christ Himself—took special measures
to open themselves up, some with rather strict methodol-
ogy. Usually in one of two ways: the first being fasting,
the second being a journey to the wilderness or desert.
Illness is another way, but this is not really a voluntary
strategy, except in the case of a few souls like Synclet-
ica of Alexandria, who devoted herself to sickness and
putrefaction to the extent that her followers had to burn
piles of incense to stand the smell of her rotting jaw.
Sickness aside, it is hard to think of anyone who has
seen visions without that lonely hunger. A forty-day fast
on Mount Verna gave St. Francis his stigmata. Elijah
heard the Lord whisper to him in the mouth of a cave.
In some other cave (saints and prophets, like bears and

rural teens, can't resist a cave), Ignatius of Loyola saw his psychedelic visions of a snake covered in eyes. Jesus Himself went to the desert to fast and pray. Then there's the Desert Fathers, who made a science of self-starvation in the wilderness of Lower Egypt.

As for the rest of us, who aren't garnished with haloes or perforated by stigmata, why wouldn't we follow in their footsteps? Why not try?

※

Twenty years ago, Paul (my priest friend, the one in Denver) and I took leave of our parishes for a week to attend a retreat in New Mexico. After flying into Albuquerque and riding a bus to some depressed desert town, the two of us waited outside a Wendy's for a shuttle to arrive and take us to the remote compound. A place where, we'd been promised by the promotional literature, we would be able to open ourselves up through a program of placid contemplation and spiritual discovery ("no matter what your tradition may be"), far from the distractions of modern life.

We sat there for three hours, killing the time watching two stray dogs fight over a bag of Cool Ranch Doritos left outside the bus station. Just as the victor yellowed his muzzle with the flavored dust of his spoils, a man from the center showed up and threw our bags into the back of his van. He wore a blue tank top flecked with drops of white paint. His teeth were like pieces of corn. A stripe of sunburn on his bare chest gave him the illusion of a long red beard.

"You ever been out here before?"

We told him we hadn't.

"Well, get ready to get addicted. You'll come back. They always do. People get hooked on these things. Gives you a buzz. People see things, and then they come back to see them again. Vortices, is what a lot of people say are out here. I used to call them 'vortexes,' but people are really specific about 'vortices.'"

Out the window: scrub and strange-looking plants, like the hands of aliens.

He used to work at another retreat center, he told us. Mostly hippies smoking weed.

"It was Transcendental. They had these meditation rooms with pads on the ceiling. Pillows. It was in case they levitated! If any of you guys wind up levitating, let me know."

He got laid off from that center, he said, because he kept cracking jokes about the place, and they had no sense of humor. But he knew someone who worked here, and she set him up with the shuttle job. They could take a joke here, he assured us.

. We arrived at the center, a small adobe building with pegs sticking out of the roof. He parked the van next to a motorcycle and a statue of a deer. The animal was misshapen—one of its legs was curled up to its chest like a snail shell, and it was clearly shorter than the other three. It made the stone animal look as if it had been mauled and was now limping its way toward death.

"I'll be the one driving you guys out there," the driver said. "I'll be watering you, too. I'll try not to mess with you too much, but sometimes I can't resist."

Paul and I thanked him and walked inside.

A woman in a leather jacket sat at one of the compound's many card tables. She looked to be about my age then, which was nearly fifty. It was her motorcycle outside. She'd ridden all the way from South Dakota, she told us. She was on a pilgrimage.

While she detailed her journey (a flock of white pelicans near Cheyenne, a stop to see the ProRodeo Hall of Fame in Colorado Springs), a young boy came into the room and sat at another one of the card tables. He ignored us completely and began playing a handheld video game. He wasn't wearing a shirt, just a pair of swim trunks with pterodactyls on them, and he put his bare feet up on the table.

The woman detailed the achievements of one of the Rodeo Hall of Fame inductees, a man who had won sixteen world championships in the various rodeo arts. She couldn't remember his name, so she kept calling him by his nickname, which was "the Babe Ruth of Rodeo."

"His name was Jim and then a body part. Jim Elbows? Jim Ankles? James Feet? He won the World All-Around Champion Cowboy Championship four years in a row," she told us with an expression of pure admiration.

Another woman appeared. She wore turquoise earrings and a Mickey Mouse T-shirt.

"Hey," she said to the boy, "you need to wear a shirt in here, or I'm going to send you over to the neighbors, where you'll fit in."

The boy sighed, got up, and left the room.

This woman poured us some water in glasses as large as cans of paint. The glasses were blue with thousands of bubbles in them, like microbes trapped in a glacier.

She introduced herself as Arena ("like a stadium") and then more or less explained to us what we already knew. Soon someone would drive us out onto the grounds, where for four days we'd sit in our meditation circles and "experience our experiences." There'd be no food (of course), but someone would be by to refill our water jugs sometime during the second day and make sure we hadn't passed out. There'd also be little lean-tos in the circles to protect us from the worst of the sun, along with first-aid kits in case we hurt ourselves. But, other than that, it was just us out there.

The boy came back with an enormous black shirt that fit him like a dress. He put his heels back up on the table.

"Feet down," Arena said. The boy sighed loudly and complied.

She asked if we had any questions.

"What do we do if we see any wild animals?" the motorcycle pilgrim asked.

"There's a whistle in the first-aid kit. Make a lot of noise and you should be able to scare most things off."

"Aren't there bears? And coyotes?"

"Bears around here are pretty meek. Coyotes don't get much bigger than forty pounds, so no worries there. They stay away from people. They're smart like that."

She handed out clipboards and pens. We signed waivers that said we couldn't sue them if we died of dehydration or were mauled by any of the animals she'd told us not to worry about, and then she led us outside.

As we walked out of the building, I noticed the barefoot boy watching us closely. His head was still angled toward his game, but his eyes, like those of a spy, followed us as we made our way toward the door. He had, by this point, somehow snatched one of our giant water glasses and brought it to his table. I was the last to leave, and just as I pulled the door shut behind me, the boy turned up the volume on his console, leaned back in his chair, and set his bare feet up on the table.

Over the course of my time in my wilderness, I saw two very strange sights. These came a few days in, once I began feeling hungry.

After our orientation, Paul, the motorcycle pilgrim, and I squeezed onto a golf cart with the shuttle driver, who dropped us off at our dusty lean-tos (each not much more than three planks and a flap of tin), which were about a mile away from each other. I was the last off.

"Last guy I brought here said he had sexual congress with a spirit. When they were done, she turned into a fountain pen. He showed me the pen. It was a Montblanc. He said I could have it, but I wasn't going to touch that thing. What if it was sticky?"

He bumped the golf cart into one of the posts, backed up, and put it in PARK.

"Okay, it's time to maroon you."

I got out. He drove away, whistling the theme song to *Gilligan's Island*.

The first day was boring, painfully so. Twice I considered getting up and walking back to the compound, but the embarrassment (before Paul, Arena, the motorcyclist, and even the barefoot boy) kept me in my circle. I inspected every inch of the lean-to, scanning for signs of previous inhabitants. I looked out at the rocks, counted my breaths, and prayed for a deer or a vulture to pop into my field of vision for a minute's entertainment.

At night I had trouble sleeping. The stars were beautiful—you could see even the most agoraphobic specks of light—but after a while I decided they were annoyingly bright. I turned my face toward one of the lean-to's posts and had a short, disappointingly literal dream that I was a rodeo clown being chased by an enormous pelican.

The second day was much like the first. I sweated through my shirt. I picked at the pimples on my arms and shoulders until I was covered in red spots. I waited for the water delivery so I could chat with the shuttle driver, a man who I didn't like much in the first place. And who, unfortunately, came that night, while I was asleep, prolonging my isolation. On that day, I did see two antelope, which leapt up and down the rocks with a teenage mischief that, to be honest, began to feel like mockery.

Then the first vision happened. It was on the third day, when my hunger was at its worst. My whole body was an empty stomach. I peeled off long splinters from the wooden posts, soaked them in the water, and chewed them like gum until they began to make my tongue bleed. Then I sucked on the blood.

I looked out and, over a slope of scrub, a few people appeared. Two or three men, more women. All completely naked, with the exception of some canteens around their necks and, in the case of one woman, a big turquoise necklace. Some had walking sticks. There was a lot of pubic hair. One man had so much it looked like he had a marmot clinging to his hips. The nudes strolled up to the shade of the rocks, set down their things, and linked hands. They began to turn, a rolling wheel.

They were middle-aged, old. Their bodies sagged and jiggled as they danced. The one with the mammal's-worth of pubes had a lot of hair on his back, too, and looked like he was dancing in a mink cape. I sat there, taking in the vision. I began to cry.

The dance was over. They walked back the way they came, vanishing behind the slope.

The next night, my last one out there, I saw the second of the visions. This time, I looked up and there, perfectly suspended in the sky, was a giant spoon. Not some ancient spoon, but the kind we had at our dinner table growing up, a plain old spoon with a slight crook in its neck and rough scrollwork at the end of the handle. I didn't know what to make of this. I just took it in to think about later. It hung there for almost an hour, fixed in place, reflecting the starlight in its polished silver. There was a good feeling to it, the way you feel when you've been driving behind the same car on the highway for hundreds of miles and, even though you know nothing

about the people in the car in front of you, you feel a connection to them. The spoon was like that.

On the drive back from our circles, Paul, the motorcycle
pilgrim, and I compared our experiences, talking volu-
bly after days of loneliness and silence.

The woman said she'd seen a deer with three heads
and antlers the size of a tree. It told her to "go to the one
her heart loved most."

"And something about zero-percent APR financ-
ing," she added. "Don't know what to make of that part.
Oh, and I remembered the name of that rodeo guy. Jim
Shoulders. Shoulders. Bugged me for the first two days,
and then came right to me on the third."

Paul said he'd seen a steep blue mountain grow
out of the ground, shooting up forever and ever, until
it poked the moon. It was covered in birds, he said. A
mountain of birds. A giant snake slithered by and melted
into a green river.

"And a pair of coyotes. Pretty sure they were real,
though. They just sat there and watched me for a while.
It definitely made things less lonely out there."

Paul would spend the rest of our trip home looking
up the birds he'd seen in a guide he bought at the airport.
Even more than me, he has always loved animals and
had some fairly heretical thoughts on them. He believed
that they, like us, were also made in God's image, that

they are more of a window into divine mystery than any pope or saint. (More than once, he railed against the suppression of the cult of St. Guinefort, a locally venerated French hound from the thirteenth century. Not exactly an orthodox view.) He made me watch nature documentaries with him, claiming there was a kind of spiritual exercise to it—the way you shift your empathy from, say, a lion, to the antelope being disemboweled by the lion, then back to the lion, had something to do with how God sees things.

It was my turn to tell them what I saw. When I shared my story about the circle of dancers, the driver, the same shuttle driver from before, began to laugh. I asked him what was so funny.

"There's a nudist colony next to the center," he said. "'Magnetic Pines' is what they're called. We've told them to stay away, but they always seem to wander onto our grounds. They're not into rules. If I have to see another old guy's dingus, I think I'll kill myself."

I remembered what the woman had said to the shirtless boy, about sending him to the neighbors, and I laughed along with the driver. But I still think it was a vision. I'm not saying those dancers weren't from a nudist colony, only that I was meant to see them. I wanted to see something strange, and I did. What difference does it make if what I saw was tangible or not?

Besides, there was still the spoon. I still had the spoon.

⚜

I passed another billboard of Jesus just west of St. Louis. A glowing white Jesus, freakishly bleached by the wind and rain. A singer-songwriter Jesus in his white karate robes. A toned, handsome, healthy, muscular, all-American Jesus.

Dionysius the Areopagite says, "We pray that we may come unto this Darkness which is beyond light, and, without seeing and without knowing, to see and to know that which is above vision and knowledge through the realization that by not-seeking and by unknowing we attain to true vision and knowledge."

John of the Cross: "Hence, when the divine light of contemplation strikes a soul not yet entirely illuminated, it causes spiritual darkness, for it not only surpasses the act of natural understanding, but it also deprives the soul of this act and darkens it."

Origen said we shouldn't picture God when we pray. In the fourth and fifth centuries, an Egyptian bishop tried to enforce this, and the reaction against him was so strong that he denounced Origen entirely. It's one of the reasons why he's not a saint.

We call this tradition the *via negativa*. The negative way. Or "by way of denial." God in the dark. God in a cloud. A God in the corner of your eye.

I agree with Origen, and everyone else. I hate the billboards. I hate that giant white cross in Effingham. I don't like holy cards all that much. Even crucifixes bother me sometimes. If anything, all my vision-seeking has only confirmed the paradox of God hiding, perfectly, in plain sight. If we want to see God in the world, all we have to do is see the world. If we want to see God in human form, look at people.

Look around. Turn around.

Billboards should be outlawed, not just the Jesus ones. They block the sky and my view of the trees.

5

I still wear the collar. I don't do this to receive any special treatment (and, given the reputation of priests in this country, it usually doesn't help much). I do it because I am a priest, and when I'm seen as one it makes me available. People see the collar and tell me their problems, recount their private miracles (their glowing orbs and sea maidens), and ask me for help. It makes the world less lonely—for them, but also for me. Especially for me.

I mention it because this happened to me last night. I was in a bar in Manhattan, Kansas, a basement dive with walls covered in pictures of famous country singers. A monochrome Tammy Wynette smiled in angelic bliss. A stern Johnny Cash smoked a cigarette as he stood in a wheat field between two large dogs. I sat hunched before the Man in Black like a supplicant. My neck and back ached from the nights in the car.

Two old men played chess in one of the booths. One of the pieces had been replaced with a key-chain Statue of Liberty. I think she was a bishop.

I drank a beer and doodled a Tammy Wynette on a coaster in the blue TV light. Another pair of men sat at the bar a few stools to my right. They were big men, meaty as Old World butchers or Irish policemen, with faces sweaty and pink like raw chicken breasts. One had eyebrows like Velcro and bowed his head penitently over his phone. The other played a bar game on a mounted touch screen, tapping it with a cigar-sized finger to pick out the subtle differences between photos of scantily clad women.

"We got it so it looks one-hundred-percent authentic," the man with the Velcro eyebrows said. "The bar is from Katie's folks' place, and it's somewhere around two hundred years old. I bought a poker table with that green felt on it off a guy in Topeka. My dad gave us that buffalo head, so I'm going to hang that up once I comb the dust out. We even got those saloon doors, but our dogs keep getting concussions on them, so we're probably going to take those off and just hang them on the wall at some point. We're saving up for a player piano, too. That's the next big buy. They're more expensive than you think."

Guy 2: "My grandma had one of those. They freak me out. She always told me it was my grandpa who was playing it, like he was a ghost. That scared the shit out of me. I knew he couldn't really play in life, but I thought maybe he'd picked it up from some other dead guy. Like Mozart or Einstein. It made me wonder why he wouldn't ever help me out from beyond the grave but, like, he could muster the ectoplasmic strength to play 'The Entertainer.'"

"She still have it? We could give her, like, three hundred."

"I don't think so. She's dead."

"That's too bad."

Each of them pulled out his own small device, a long USB key, and sucked on the end. A few seconds later, they both let out clouds of steam from their mouths and noses, like angry cartoon bulls.

A woman came over and sat beside me. She looked to be about fifty or so, and her forearms were covered in indistinct tattoos, a map of black islands I couldn't quite make out.

"You're a priest?"

I told her I was.

"Do you work around here?"

I explained that I was technically retired, and that I was traveling to see some friends.

"When you retire, do they take away your powers? Like, can you say a service? Or do a Communion?"

"Once you're a priest, you're always a priest."

"How long have you been in the game?"

"Almost fifty years."

"Did you have a calling? Isn't that what you call it? It'd be so much easier for God to show up and just tell you what to do with your life like that. I wish I had that. What was that like?"

"It's a boring story."

All of a sudden everyone in the bar began to cough. A wave of fits moved through us, making us honk like a flock of geese.

"Something in the air," one of the large men said.

The coughing let up. She bought me another beer. She said she'd had a lot on her mind. She'd been thinking about going to confession for a while now, and then here I was. A sign. She'd been dreaming about her parents a lot in the past year or so, and couldn't shake off the thought of them.

"Are you close with your family?" she asked.

"Yeah. We're all pretty close."

She hadn't talked to her parents for years before they died. But lately she'd been carrying them around with her every day. It was like her head was a haunted house, she told me.

There were two moments in particular that really got to her.

"I used to call them when I was on coke and just talk and talk, and then they'd try to come over and I'd lock the door. I'd chain it, too, with a big boat chain. A Jacob Marley chain." She measured out the thickness between her fingers. "One morning, I came outside and my mom had written 'I love you' in lipstick on my door. And I was all, like, fuck that. And then, a year or so later—this is the second thing—when I lied and told her I'd gotten clean, my mom had given me a job at her office (she was an accountant)—I'd broken into the office and I stole some of the computers and office equipment and sold them and didn't show up for work after that. I stole my dad's Triumph and moved out here—I'm from Dayton, Ohio—and now they're dead and I have no one to apologize to. I can't really make it up to them. They were good to me, and then they died before I figured out how shitty I'd been. So what I really want to do is to make a confession. Can I do that?"

"Sure."

"Do you think you could just do it here? Should we step outside? Or, like, get a booth?"

I looked around at the booths and the pantheon of country singers with their serene, saintly faces.

"I think we can just do it here."

"Do I need to say it again?"

I told her one time was good enough. "Are you truly sorry?"

"I am. I'm really sorry."

I said the old words and made the sign of the cross over her, and I told her she had to go do something good for someone else as a penance. I didn't feel I had to be specific. I figured she'd find the right penance to make herself feel better about things.

"Thanks. I actually do feel better. Kind of lightweight."

I felt better, too. I probably should have directed

her to an actual church, but I craved the company. She made me feel useful, like a screwdriver or a stepladder.

She looked over to the little stage at the back of the bar.

"Hey, I got this new thing. Want to try it?"

She walked me over to the stage and pulled out a black box. A karaoke machine.

"Are we allowed?"

"We are if I say so. I'm the owner."

She turned it on, picked a song for herself from a thick white binder, and pulled out the corresponding CD. She dug around in a drawer and fished out a golden microphone. I suddenly felt like a foreign dignitary in an autocrat's court.

She chose Glen Campbell's "Wichita Lineman." Her voice was surprisingly strong and soulful. She tilted her head back and opened her mouth so wide I thought she might pull one of the muscles in her face. She looked like the MGM lion.

I am a lineman for the county
And I drive the main road . . .

When she finished, she held the microphone in front of her chest like a trophy. One of the bartenders gave his employer an obligatory clap, and a few of the barflies took the hint and joined in.

"Now you go."

I looked through the selection. The songs only went up to the year 2000. I picked Prince's "Purple Rain," which was one of the only Prince songs it had.

While I sang, the woman swayed back and forth. For the last verse, she pulled a green lighter out of her pocket and held the flame high above her head. Everyone else, thankfully, ignored me.

"Clap for him!" she ordered into the golden mic when I was done, and her court of employees and regulars gave me a quick salvo of mandatory applause.

"What an emotional rendition," she told me when I was done. "You were really feeling it! You can tell. That's one of the most important parts of singing—after hitting the notes. Was it me, or were you almost about to cry?"

"I guess I just put my heart into it."

"You deserve a Tony. Or, like, an Emmy. Or at least a Golden Globe. Golden Globes are doable."

We drank our beers, and I watched one of the big men at the bar pick out the differences between two pictures of the same girl in a bikini and cowboy boots riding a horse. One of the girls had a nose ring.

Every sacrament has every other sacrament in it. Baptism reconciles original sin. Confirmation renews baptism. Communion is a marriage of the Body of Christ to itself, a marriage that cleanses us of sin (at least the venal variety). Last rites are confession, Eucharist, and baptism together all in one. We sat there, drinking, and made her confession a Eucharist as Johnny Cash glowered over us like the cranky God of the Old Testament.

The first time I performed a baptism I was a co-celebrant, freshly assigned to St. Antony's. The pastor (whose job I'd have a couple years later), said the words and dipped the baby in the water as the parents, the godparents, and I stood around. But when he went to smear the baby's head with oil, the infant whipped her arm around and slapped him right on his head. Everyone laughed, including me, but afterward the pastor told me that the slap meant something that I should think about when I christen a child on my own. In blessing we are blessed. When we administer the sacraments, those who take them—the penitent, the communicant, the bride, or the groom—they are the ones who sanctify us. In giving these things, we receive their holiness. It is in pardoning that we are pardoned, etc. It was a good lesson, and I think about it every time I do a baptism.

Or every time I used to do a baptism. I don't know if I'll ever get to do another.

My new friend pointed to the back of the bar, where, between a few near-empty bottles of brown liquid, hung a strange little pistol, mounted like the bric-a-brac at the Cracker Barrel.

"I bought that in a parking lot when I was nineteen,

with sixty-two dollars I stole from my parents. I can't keep it in my house, because it kept showing up in my dreams. But if I throw it away it's kind of like I'm throwing away something they gave me. So I put it here."

She went behind the bar and ripped it right out of its frame.

"The handle's real human bone, from a femur. See the head? They carved a skull into it."

She grabbed it by the nose and held it in front of my face. The handle was much longer than the stubby barrel. The bone had been cut about a third of the way down, so that the butt consisted of a few inches of the shaft and the knob where the bone fits into the hip socket. The skull carved into this knob was crude and smoothed down from wear. The artist had tried to incorporate the hole at the end of the bone into one of the eyeholes, which gave you the impression it was winking at you like a dirty old man. As for the lethal end, it was no bigger than a glue gun. The whole thing weighed about as much as a hammer.

She handed the pistol over to me.

"Could you take it? Find a good place to bury it? Say a prayer or something?"

The gun smelled sour, like stale beer, and had the electric feeling that only holy or forbidden things give off. I'd been fantasizing about buying one, eyeing the Bass Pro Shops and Cabela's off the highway, but I didn't think I'd work up the courage to pull over. And now here one was, a sign.

I put the derringer in my bag.

I told her I'd found a stray dog and asked her if she knew where in town I could find an animal shelter. She copied the directions onto a coaster for me.

"Well, that's good of you. What kind of dog is it?" she asked.

"A mutt," I said. "Some little stray."

"I can relate."

One more thing on the sacraments.

For the Jubilee Year in 2000, I organized a service at the convention center with a rabbi and a Methodist. At one point, the Methodist asked me to do something—I forget just what, some Methodist thing—and I told him I wasn't comfortable performing a ritual if I didn't know its meaning.

"We don't do it because we know what it means," he said. "We do it to find out what it means."

I first met Paul when we were both students at John Bosco's, in Indiana. Years later, long after we'd lost touch, I received a call from him and learned that, through some ecclesiastical coincidence, he'd been posted to a church in a nearby diocese, about a three-hour drive south of mine. We arranged to meet soon after, and our friendship picked up right where we'd left off.

Our tendencies being less conservative than the other priests in the state, we were natural allies and grew close immediately. We went on retreats together, like the one in New Mexico, and his gift of Thomas Merton's *The Wisdom of the Desert* was what originally turned me on to the Desert Fathers. Paul was always better read than me—he's also the one who first introduced me to my favorite passage by the Venerable Bede:

"When we compare the present life of man on earth with that time of which we have no knowledge, it seems to me like the swift flight of a single sparrow through the banqueting hall where you are sitting at dinner on a winter's day. . . ." He describes the fire going, the dark winter storms raging outside. Bede's sparrow flies swiftly in through one door, out the other. Darkness, a brief interruption of orange heat, darkness. While he's inside, he's safe from the rain and cold, but after a few moments of comfort, he vanishes from sight "into the wintry world from which he came."

Paul performed the Mass when my mother died, and the year after that I took leave to drive him to Wisconsin to help him bury his brother. In those tough years, we were there for each other, and I still believe that, were it not for his friendship, I might have quit the priesthood altogether.

By the early 2000s, thanks in part to a national priest shortage that left us without any associates to share the workload, we found ourselves taking on more duties and making fewer and fewer trips to see each other. Still, his friendship was very real to me, and even when we weren't in touch, it had a solid presence; it was an amulet I could hold when my life felt empty and endless. We didn't have to be in contact for it to mean something.

Then, one day, he showed up in my office. He wore a denim jacket, jeans, and a denim shirt. No collar. He said he had a lot to tell me, so I poured him a cup of coffee and we sat down.

In the prime of our friendship, it wasn't unusual for one of us to appear uninvited or unannounced. That was part of our relationship, adding some surprise to the otherwise routine life of a parish priest. But this time, I knew something was going on.

Paul sipped his coffee and stared at my copy of Merton's *The Wisdom of the Desert*, which he'd pulled off the bookshelf when he arrived. He had a dramatic streak and liked to plant a drawn-out silence before he told me something important. I knew some kind of announcement was coming and rode it out until he started talking.

He told me that three years ago, while organizing an interfaith retreat, he'd met a Unitarian minister and felt a special connection. He thought it had been the beginning of a close friendship, something like ours, but it was another thing entirely. To put it plainly, he was in love. Deeply in love with this minister, a man, and he wanted me to meet him. He wanted me to meet him because he wanted me to officiate their wedding.

"It won't be a Mass, don't worry. And it'll be in Massachusetts, to get some distance. I just want you to do it."

This brings me to one of the many frustrations of this life. You get asked to do the baptism, but not to be a godfather. You officiate the wedding, but you're never asked to be a groomsman. You execute the funeral, but you can't mourn among the mourning. You may stand in the middle of things, but you're really on the outside, an extra in the movie, not much more than a prop.

I didn't have any issue with Paul's sexuality. I'd long suspected he was gay and was fine with that. We were celibate, and although that doesn't erase your sexuality, it does relegate it to a small part of your life, at least for me. A room in your house you never step inside, really. A parlor with the furniture wrapped in plastic. What hurt me wasn't that he'd found love, but that he was giving up the priesthood. And that breaking this solemn vow seemed little more than an afterthought to him. I suppose I felt betrayed, too, given how close we'd been in our early years as priests.

"Are you okay?" Paul asked me.

"I'm really happy for you. Just a little shocked, I guess."

I asked about his plans to leave his parish, and he said he was going to be a Unitarian minister, might even go back to get a master's in divinity in Chicago. He returned to the question of my officiation.

"Will you do it? Will you think about it?"

I told him that I was flattered but that I'd have to think it over, and then we talked for a while about his partner and just how he would go about explaining things to his parish. It was almost like back when we were close, and so, when he checked his watch and told me it was about time for him to make the drive home, I had the urge to invite him to stay over in the rectory. It wasn't the old days, though. He'd chosen a new life, and I needed to let him go.

He got up to leave, but he stood there for a moment before walking out. Another one of his thespian pauses. I waited.

But he didn't say anything this time. He put *The*

Wisdom of the Desert back on the shelf, gave me a hug, and left.

Even though Paul's wedding was long after I allowed the wake of the Romany king to take place at the church, I was nevertheless still on rough ground with the bishop. The wake was just the beginning of a series of misunderstandings and, if I can be frank, some overreaching on his part. He was a pre–Vatican II guy. He disliked the austerity of our worship space, and (as if predicting my expulsion from my last rectory) greatly disapproved of my efforts to include the practices of other faiths into the spiritual life of the congregation. As I considered my friend's invitation, I told myself that, were I to be directly involved in this in any way, the bishop would certainly find out, and there'd be a high likelihood I'd be removed from my parish and position. I also think that, in all honesty, I did feel abandoned. My friend had found a new life and left me alone.

Two days later, I called Paul and told him that, owing to the ongoing drama between me and the bishop, I couldn't officiate, but that I would certainly go to the service. He told me he understood, but I knew him well enough to hear the disappointment in his voice.

So I went to Boston, that Catholic capital of America, to attend the ceremony in a Unitarian church. The interior looked so much like mine back home that it made me feel uneasy almost immediately. Hexagonal, nearly in the round, without much ornament. Chairs, not pews, with a few abstract pieces here and there. Were it any closer in resemblance to my church, I'd have suspected Paul was taunting me, and maybe I was inclined to believe he was.

I took my seat, and soon the music began. My friend had found someone else to officiate, but Paul's participation dominated the ceremony. He summoned the pianist to her bench. He cued the lectors. The officiant kept looking over to the groom, who stood like a coach on the sidelines, calling the plays. Twice I thought I saw Paul mouthing the words of the liturgy (or pseudo-liturgy, really). He was still a priest, I thought. He would never not be one.

Don't get me wrong. I found the ceremony very moving, and I was proud of my friend for knowing what he was meant to do and doing it. I'm still proud of him.

He sent me a letter that I still keep on my car's console. Its green envelope is tattooed with his crude cartoons, drawings of castles and moons. On the back he'd sketched a mountain covered in birds—cockatoos, storks, vultures, flamingos—that takes up the whole rectangle.

Of all the thing I've done, I think refusing to help

my friend is one of the whetstones that will remain around my neck when I die. That, and what happened with Bruno. If Origen is right and what we do in this age determines our form in the next, then at best I'll come back as a dog, or be reborn the exact way I am now.

7

The woman at the shelter recognized the coyote for what it was right away. I'd brought her out to the car to show her, just so I wouldn't have to move the coyote around so much if she wound up turning him away. Which is what she did.

"You wrapped his leg?"

I nodded.

"Wow. He's a scrawny little dude. Looks like a juvenile. So—I can give you a carrier, but we can't take in wild animals. Let me show you something."

The shelter was loud with the dogs barking in their narrow cells. Many of the animals had short brown or pink fur that made them look like they were covered in human skin. She pointed out a pen in the back where a large husky was curled up.

"That's a wolf-dog," she said as she handed me the carrier. "They're pretty popular nowadays. We're getting a lot of these in here."

She looked at the creature with fear and awe.

"The other dogs, even the meanest ones, can sense him. You can tell they know something is more intense about him. I think they can smell it. I can smell it. We have to euthanize him. All of the wolf-dogs. They're too dangerous. Everybody wants a tame wild animal. But dogs are tame wild animals. Wolves, and wolf hybrids, are plain old wild animals. So are coyotes. Wild animals aren't supposed to be pets. It's kind of arrogant, no offense."

"It's not my pet. I'm just trying to find a place for him."

"You should take him to Animal Control. Or find a wildlife refuge. I know one you can go to. You have a phone?"

I pulled out my phone. It's the kind you flip open, and when I did that, a couple yellowed receipts gently tumbled down to the floor like dead leaves.

"Okay, I'll just write the address down for you."

※

Growing up, I often wished I had been raised by wolves or panthers, like Mowgli in *The Jungle Book*. More than that, I wanted to be transformed into a wild animal. When I was five, I misheard a story about Jesus healing a leper. Having no knowledge of Hansen's disease, I heard "leopard." Jesus had, in my understanding, turned a leopard into a human. The language of "cleansing," I assumed, had to do with the spots. The standing upright made sense, too, I figured, since now the cat was bipedal. I had my sister read me the story until she got sick of it. I wanted to be a leopard. If a leopard could become human, then surely I could be turned into a leopard, if I prayed hard enough. I imagined the spots falling off the cat like dirt in the bathtub. I re-enacted the scene with one of my oldest sister's polka-dot dresses, wrapping myself in the skirt and crouching on the floor, then shaking it off and standing upright in front of the mirror, looking at my hands in wonder as if they were suddenly new. Fingers! Thumbs! And then I reversed, pulling the dress back over myself as I returned to my feline squat.

I carried the story around until I told it to one of my brothers, who corrected me and wrote out both words in the margins of the newspaper. "Leper" and "leopard." I moped around the house for days, staring out the window and up into the treetops. I wanted to be a leopard.

The woman's desk was covered in flashcards with the names of different body parts. She drew a map on one of the cards, with a couple wobbly county roads traced around the word "ileum."

"I'm pre-med," she explained, and handed it to me along with a bottle of dog tranquilizers, which I tossed in the carrier.

I thought I'd take one last look at the wolf. Now the animal rested its head on its hind legs and I could see its huge face. The same wildness was in its eyes as in the coyote's.

"Dogs and coyotes and wolves can all interbreed," she told me. "A lot of coyotes have some wolf and dog in them somewhere."

I thanked the girl and left.

Before driving off, I smeared some leftover Spam along the back of the carrier, to lure the coyote inside. Once I'd placed the crate next to him, he looked over my obvious trap, took a few weak sniffs, then went back to sleep. I used a bungee to keep the wire door open and hoped he'd climb in when he was hungry.

I tried to follow the directions to Animal Control, but I got turned around on the highway. I pulled over to get my bearings and saw the coyote had crawled into the crate. I'd find a place for him somewhere else, I told myself, and kept on going west.

8

The gun smelled about as bad as the coyote. A yeasty smell, as if it'd been baptized in beer every night for many soggy decades. Both the metal and the bone were covered in a pointillistic film of grease. I took an exit and filled my bucket with warm water in the rest-stop bathroom. Back at the car, I added a squirt of the Dawn dish soap I use to sanitize the bucket, and, with a rag and a few Q-tips, set to work removing the thick coat of grime from the derringer.

Standing over the hood, I felt a strange sensation, an unexpected flow of muscle memory. My arms and hands took over and buffed out the stubborn smudges. Only when I started wiping the barrel down and drying off the butt did I recognize it: the feeling of polishing the chalice and cruets in the sacristy.

It made sense. The derringer had come to me by way of a sacrament, if an improvised one. But I didn't want it to be blessed with that power. If anything, I wanted the opposite. What was that? A curse, maybe.

Pulling myself out of sacerdotal autopilot, I dropped the derringer. It bounced off the hood and rolled into the dirt. I picked it back up and started all over again.

࿊

There used to be eight deadly sins, not just seven. They cut one out somewhere. I don't know why. Evagrius of Pontus, one of my favorite desert monks, documented eight, but I guess someone thought seven was a better number. The one they cut was called "acedia." The noonday demon. "Listlessness" might be a word for it, but I don't think that's quite right. John Cassian describes it pretty well in his *Institutes*:

> When this besieges the unhappy mind, it begets aversion from the place, boredom with one's cell, and scorn and contempt for one's brethren, whether they be dwelling with one or some way off, as careless and unspiritually minded persons. Also, towards any work that may be done within the enclosure of our own lair, we become listless and inert. It will not suffer us to stay in our cell, or to attend to our reading: we lament that in all this while, living in the same spot, we have made no progress, we sigh and complain that bereft of sympathetic fellowship we have no spiritual fruit; and bewail ourselves as empty of all spiritual profit, abiding vacant and useless in this place; and we that could guide others and be of value to multi-

tudes have edified no man, enriched no man with our precept and example.

They shouldn't have cut this one. It's the perfect word for what I feel now, driving around in my car-cell. The farther I drive forward, the more the demon shows up to make me look back, telling me I've made no progress. I have no spiritual fruit.

If I close my eyes and try to picture him, the noonday demon incarnate, Bruno stares back at me with his basketball-round head, the pins on his lapel gleaming, his collar pure white and shining, like a false tooth.

I almost didn't join the priesthood. There were a couple times when the thought of it lacked any appeal at all, even though I was well on my way to ordination. My first period of doubt happened early on, when I was in the minor seminary. I was sixteen.

The same variety of religious experience that led me to the priesthood almost turned me away from it. Since I was ten, I've suffered from unusual headaches. The first came when we were living outside of Fort Wayne, in a suburb near the reservoir. I was out in our yard, digging a hole with a stick in the dirt, either burying one of my toys (something I did all the time, entombing tin soldiers, plastic horses, broken yo-yos that had fallen valiantly in the line of duty), or digging it back up again to resurrect it. Whatever it was, when I finished and looked away from the hole I'd dug, it was still there, floating in my field of vision. Everywhere I looked, the hole was there. It shrank to the size of a jelly bean, but it stayed right in the middle of my sight. When I tried to read a book, the hole was on the pages. I tried to look at my sister, but her face was gone. It wasn't a real hole, exactly. It was more like the world was a curtain, and someone had pinched away some of it on the other side and wrapped that tiny bundle up in a rubber band. I was looking at an absence. After a while, it faded away and I had a terrible headache.

This happened again, about once a year after that, with different symptoms. One time, I couldn't see faces: I could look at an eye, a nose, or a mouth, but I couldn't fit them together. It was like my brothers' and sisters' faces were sentences, and I knew all the words they contained, but couldn't make any sense of them. Other times, I saw light coming off of people's bodies (yellow light, occasionally pink), or I might lose three or four hours in a blurry trance, with half the day disappearing behind me in what felt like a minute or two.

By the time I was at St. John Bosco's, I was used to this. I knew they were neurological misfires, but I also thought they gave me a special connection to my heroes, my Beatles of the Communion of Saints. St. Ignatius (probably Paul, the disciplined stoner) had his trippy visions in the caves of Manresa. Teresa of Avila (my brainy, wild John) had her terrible migraines and terrific ecstasies. John of the Cross (diffident George) and Francis (lovable Ringo). All of them had the same—if much more grand and consequential—cocktail of illness, depression, and illumination. Though I knew I wasn't special like them, I was grateful to peek into something that might be a little holy, a glimpse into some other life beyond my life. I think my first religious instincts were partly born in these bizarre headaches and can be traced back to the holes in the world they made. Or showed.

But then, one day, when I was sixteen, I had an especially bad one. It was another void, this time a tiny bean right in front of me, erasing numbers on a clock or the words in my catechism. When I explained my situation to one of the priests, he sent me to the dormitory to ride it out. But instead of the usual headache, the left half of my body went numb. The right side of my head felt tingly, settling into a long brain-freeze. I couldn't remember my name or my phone number. I went to the nurse—or tried to, because I got lost in the hallway. I walked into the laundry room, full of black cassocks scattered on the floor like shadows. I thought I was having a stroke. I thought to myself: This is it. I am going to die, or at least part of me is going to die, so that the me that I know now will no longer exist, which is certainly a kind of death. What was worse was that I didn't feel God anywhere inside that. There was no peace, only panic and terror.

It wore off, and in a couple hours I was more or less fine. Mentally, I was fine. Spiritually, I was in crisis. Where was God? Where were Jesus and Mary at the hour of my death, so to speak? Daily Mass felt hollow. Prayer was like tossing pennies into the sea. I had trouble sleeping and spent my nights walking off my restlessness on the grounds of the seminary. Late one night, as I wandered through the library in my insomniac despair, I came across *The Cloud of Unknowing.* I was drawn to the hippie image of the title and started reading.

Written by some anonymous medieval priest, the book instructs the practice of imageless prayer for young priests and monks. *The Cloud* paints a portrait (or unpaints, I guess) of a deeply mysterious God beyond language. It was my first encounter with the *via negativa.* Reading it, and trying it, I felt it was true. Not only that, but I felt the love of the anonymous author, reaching across time to help me with my spiritual edification. Whoever he was, he was a spiritual genius. Which is to say, a kind of artist.

I decided I'd follow the program set forth by the mysterious author, and for weeks I'd sneak off to the woods behind the school and practice. Though I'd found the book in the seminary library, it had the feeling of contraband, even heresy. Had I been found out by one of my teachers, he would have been fine with it, yet I knew that any discovery of my program would drain *The Cloud* of its secret energy.

The second or third time I tried it, I felt like I got high. I can say this from experience, because during my time at the seminary it was not completely uncommon for my friends to procure pot. In fact, Paul and I had access to a seemingly limitless supply of weed, along with a few other hallucinogenic drugs every now and then. By this I mostly mean mushrooms or the occasional sheet of acid. We'd take small doses before Mass and sit there, grinning like goons, through the liturgy as stained-glass saints swayed high above us and the organ music looped around our heads in bright streams. Our teachers occasionally remarked on our sincere devotion, and their favor gave us even more leeway to slip away and get higher.

But by this point Paul had left, a brief hiatus before returning to his vocation, and his absence, I think, certainly contributed to my despair.

I went to the woods with the same delinquent spirit, carrying *The Cloud* like it was a bag of weed, and when I walked back out, the sky seemed to be taller, and higher. The border between me and everything around me— my fellow seminarians, the priests, the groundskeeper, even the cafeteria tables and foam ceiling tiles—seemed permeable and artificial. Though most of this buzz wore off by the next morning, there was always a faint residue that stuck around, building up after each session like a new coat of paint.

After finishing my medieval program, I decided to remain on my path toward the priesthood, and since then, *The Cloud* has led me to a trove of other spiritual texts—the writings of Dionysius the Areopagite, the Spiritual Exercises of St. Ignatius, Thomas Merton, Simone Weil, Julian of Norwich. It follows that it is also at the root of why I no longer live at the rectory, why I now live in a Toyota Camry.

The migraines let up in my early forties. They came less and less, and then they stopped. That was around when I began seeking out other kinds of spiritual experimentation. The wilderness retreats, the programs in meditation and contemplation, my metalwork and dome building. The headaches were, from the start, mostly unpleasant, if not downright frightening. But now I want them back. I miss them.

The second time I considered leaving was after a wave of sex-abuse allegations. It came out that for years a priest in a nearby diocese had been raping two boys in his congregation. Bruno. I read about it in the newspaper. Not long after that, I read the articles by *The Boston Globe* and I felt complicit. This was 2002. I was still at my parish at the time. I lied and said I was sick for a week, and they brought in someone else to say Mass.

I laid in my room for those seven days, and every morning I considered leaving. What good was the Church? In the end, had the institutional church done more evil than good? I tried tallying things up. Christian colonies in New Spain had murdered and raped hundreds of thousands, if not millions, of people. Priests owned slaves (see the Jesuits of nineteenth-century Virginia). The Inquisition, the massacres of Jews, the racist violence of the Crusades—all of this was done for Christendom and with the help of people in collars and stoles. People like me. Children had been raped. Dictatorships kept in place. And weren't the Catholics I loved fringe figures anyway? Dorothy Day, the author of *The Cloud*, Archbishop Romero, Merton . . .

Of course, I'd known all these things for a long time. I'd pushed them back, into some dank dungeon in my head, and now the scandal had opened the door and let them all come screaming out.

What, then, was my responsibility to God? Which is to say, what was my responsibility to His children, my brothers and sisters, and *actual children*?

But I had taken a vow, I reminded myself, and that

meant something. I decided it was my role to remain on the edge of the outside of things. I would be a parish priest, but from that point on I wouldn't accept any more duties, and if I was transferred somewhere else, I'd no longer wish to be a pastor.

A few years later, when I received a call asking if I wanted to be the bishop of the Diocese of Evansville, I told them I'd thought and prayed about it and I had to refuse. Not long after that, the bishop of my diocese began tightening his grip in what was, for most of the country, a renaissance for conservative Catholics and, for those of us with less fondness for the nineteenth century, a period of soft voices and hushed opinions, a sad and silent crisis in which the pre–Vatican II and Eisenhower priests held sway and the pot-smoking, guitar-playing, meditating priests stayed in hiding. It was, I can see now, the beginning of the end for me.

As for Father Bruno, he's living at a communal residence for retired priests in St. Ignatius, Montana.

I poured the soapy water into the drainage ditch. I'd done a good job with the gun. This second time, I didn't resist my sacristy reflex and polished it like a chalice. The smell was mostly gone, and the steel shone the white sunlight back so brightly it was hard to look at. All I needed now was ammunition. I was in the right part of the country for that.

Before I got back on the road, I called a number I'd copied on Paul's envelope back in Indiana. An ancient secretary answered. The connection was weak. Her voice came through a veil of hiss and fog. From the sound of it, she might've been taking a shower on a submarine.

"Hi. My name is William O'Rourke," I lied, using the name of a priest from my former diocese. "I'm trying to get in touch with an old friend, James Bruno, and I was told he might be living in Ignatius. Is that right? Just want to make sure before I come all that way." Even to lie that we were friends upset me.

"Yep. Father Bruno's here. Should I let him know he should be expecting a visitor?"

"No. I want to surprise him."

9

The coyote and I made our way through the middle of Kansas. He was getting more active, which I thought was good. His eyes followed me through the wire door of the carrier as I rearranged my things in the back seat. I could hear his tail drum against the sides of the box when I stopped for gas. Occasionally, he let out a trombony fart, which, despite the rank, beef-jerky stench, I took as a sign that his system was beginning to work properly. My plan now was to find a place for him when I visited Paul in Colorado. I was inclined to think they'd be nicer to him in Colorado.

Where I grew up, they'd pay you a quarter for a pair of coyote ears. My brothers took me coyote hunting all the time. We laid traps in the copse of silver maple by the quarry. We shot at them from old deer stands, or we built our own out of scrap wood and staked out our prey up there for hours, silently waiting for one to trot by, our only means of communication a notepad and pencil on which we drew obscene cartoons. I liked the target practice, but when it came time to pounce on our quarry, I mostly watched. Once, my brother made me cut the ears off one, but I cried after the first ear, and he finished the other. For some reason, that was harder than watching it get shot. It was common in our town to see boys carrying strings of coyote ears and tails on wires and old coat hangers, ready to fly their brutal kites. My suspicion was that Kansas was like that, too, and that the hippies in Colorado would be more in favor of wildlife conservation. If I were a coyote, that would be the place I would want to spend my days of sniffing and chasing rabbits or whatever coyotes do in the woods when no one is watching.

Out there the grass was coyote-colored. It was late summer, and everything looked like it was carved out of cork. As I drove along 70, I heard a terrifying grinding sound, like a chicken bone stuck in a garbage disposal. I checked my mirrors and, seeing no other cars around, slowed down the Camry so I could better make out the source.

A horn blared. Out of nowhere, a truck sped past me on my left. A teenage girl flipped me off as the truck went by.

Still, I'd slowed enough for things to quiet down, and once the truck was gone I determined that the sound was coming from the crate.

Before I left the shelter, I'd stupidly set the crate behind the driver's seat, which meant that now I couldn't see inside without leaning across the center console and craning my neck. A maneuver tricky enough for me on its own, made all the more difficult by the added task of steering the car.

I checked the mirrors again. The truck was a ways up the road now, a blue postage stamp in the distance.

I leaned over and tried to see what was going on. But getting a good look inside was harder than I'd thought. Even when I leaned back as far as I could and twisted my neck, I still couldn't see anything.

Another horn. I jerked up. The muscles in my neck spasmed. Balancing out my contorted lean, I'd put too much of my weight on the gas. I was right behind the truck this time, and they swerved into the other lane to avoid me. I slowed back down, and they sped up and passed me again. I saw the girl for a second time, mouthing the words "What the fuck?" and waving her hands in the universal sign of bewildered rage.

I turned on my hazards, pulled over, got out, and opened the rear door to see what was going on. I'd pulled something in my neck when I leaned over, and now I couldn't turn my head to the left. From then on, I told myself, I'd make sure always to set the carrier on the other side so I could peek in without killing anyone.

The coyote scrutinized me through the grate with his orange eyes. He'd chewed right through one of the links on the door, leaving two twisted prongs jutting toward him. His teeth were pink with blood. But what struck me most were his ears.

This coyote had huge ears, the kind you see on those desert foxes in *National Geographic*, those catlike foxes that eat termites and need the big bat ears so they can hear all the way through the ground. They would've been worth extra had my brother and I turned them in. The whole world would change if we had ears like that, or the noses of dogs, or the eyes of eagles or houseflies. The whole thing would be completely unrecognizable.

Another Christ, crucified on a billboard back in Lenexa. The president staring at me from the front page of a newspaper in a Lawrence gas station—he's Bruno-like, with his stiff yellow doll-hair and his lunch-meat face. Jesus on a bumper sticker on the back of a truck on 70, beside the words "REMEMBER, I AM WATCHING YOU." The president on TV in a Junction City diner, his face puffed and angry like a cartoon thundercloud on the edge of a map. There's more Bruno-ness here, too, not just in the blood-filled face or the hair, but in the beady eyes, the lurching, neckless head. The next Jesus outside a church in Abilene, fifty feet tall, seemingly carved out of soap or sugar. The president on another bumper sticker, his name above that of his vice-president (my old governor, my former congressman), the sticker above

another, the outline of a rifle with a long barrel and a
thick stock. Jesus painted on a barn near Salina, his eyes
blue and wide, his mouth as big as a canoe, his teeth precisely the same size and shape as tombstones.

My country is a bad church. A church of itself.

10

This afternoon, as I sped past the shaggy farms of western Kansas, I saw a billboard for a peculiar roadside attraction.

MARTIN'S HOLE TO HELL.
WORLD-FAMOUS BOTTOMLESS PIT
NEXT EXIT.

Under the words were painted a gang of devils dancing around a black circle. The devils were probably red at one point, but rain and sun had paled them to bubble-gum pink.

When the exit came, I took it and began to follow the signs leading to the pit. They, like the billboard, were old and faded, hand-painted decades ago and left to chip and wear away.

After a while, with no sign of a sign, I was ready to turn around when I saw the last arrow, pointing me to the bottomless pit.

There's something oddly medieval about American roadside attractions. They are the great-(great-great-great, etc.) grandchildren of the enterprising shrines along the old *via*s, peddling their relics to high-speed pilgrims, telling them they have only to stop for a while to stick their feet in the strange currents of mystery. I'd been tempted by a few already—a giant concrete prairie dog, a hall of fame for greyhound racers—but this one, with its small gesture toward the infinite, I couldn't resist.

The hole was, apparently, on someone's farm. I followed the dirt path up a gentle slope, through tall yellow grass on both sides. Grasshoppers took off to get out of my way, though many, instead of escaping the van, leapt out from the safety of the brush and bounced off the hood and windshield, popping like hail.

Since I picked up the gun, I'd begun to doubt my course of action, and thought I should simply avoid the stop in Montana altogether and go straight from Denver to Seattle, as planned. Somewhere over the course of the past fifty miles, the derringer's aura had turned sinister, emitting its demonic radioactivity from the glove compartment. The Hole to Hell seemed like a sign, or at least the beginning of one, a place where I could stop and take stock of things. Maybe I'd drop the derringer in.

Halfway up the hill, I slammed the brakes. A dirty brown dog sat in the middle of the driveway. It looked at me, only vaguely interested in the car a few feet in front of it. I tapped the horn, but the dog didn't budge. I inched closer, hoping it would back off, but the dog still wouldn't move.

It didn't growl or bark. Its tail twitched occasionally, but didn't wag.

I kept inching the car closer, and finally the dog stalked off into the grass.

I parked on a gravel patch by a barn. The side of the barn was painted with the words "BOTTOMLESS PIT," but someone had graffitied a few additions that had turned PIT into BITCH.

Before stepping out of the car, I made sure to crack the windows for the coyote. I left him some water in the carrier, too, along with a scoop of tuna fish from a can I'd picked up at one of the gas stations. I took the der-ringer with me in case the opportunity to fling it into the pit presented itself.

Up by the house, a man stood next to a lawn mower. He'd seen me pull in, and parked the mower under a tree before walking down the hill. I stood there waiting, next to a collection of old farm equipment, a garden of rusty coils and fearsome blades.

"Can I help you?" the man asked.

I told him I'd come for the pit.

"Really? Damn." He shook my hand and intro-duced himself as Martin.

"From the billboard," I said.

"No. No, that's my dad. He's dead. Thank God. Not many people've come out to see the pit since he was alive. And few did even back then."

He wore a purple Kansas State University baseball cap, which he took off and loosened to reveal a shiny strait of scalp between the hair on the sides of his head.

"Well, shall we?"

He walked me to the pit. The dog followed behind, down the long path to a lot behind the house.

The pit had been there as long as anyone could remember, Martin told me. His great-granddad had purchased the land from a Kiowa man in the 1880s, and the hole had come with it. It was probably just an old well, but his father (who had also been the Ellsworth County postmaster) had dumped a bunch of money into it—not literally, though it might as well have been— after they built the highway.

Halfway down, I turned and saw the dog. It'd stopped some twenty yards back and now sat there, tracking our progress.

Martin turned.

"Reese Witherspoon always gets spooked by the pit. Dad liked to tell people he fell in and that's why he won't go near it. But really Reese was always like that." He turned back to the dog and hollered, "*You pussy!*"

"That's an odd name for a dog."

"She was my wife's favorite actor. My kid's, too. I didn't have much of a say. She really is a good actor, though. You ever see *Election*?"

We reached the lot, where another old hand-painted

sign stood by a circle of charred fence posts. The pit, roughly the size of a hula hoop, was right in the middle of the posts.

The sign read "HOLE TO HELL!" with a gang of red devils poking the letters with pitchforks. Someone had drawn women's breasts and giant penises on a few of them in black marker. Teenagers everywhere draw dicks onto everything. It's their American flag, their cross.

"Dad was always trying to get me to join in the business. When I was six or seven, he made me sell lemonade with red food coloring in it. He called it Demonade. Demonade. You could taste the red in it. It had a flavor if you added too much."

He kicked some fallen tree branches around.

"Take a look," he said.

I peeked over the posts and looked into the hole, folding myself over to spare the tender muscles in my neck. Past its fringe of yellow grass there was a crown of brown clay that went about four feet down. Not much farther below that it was a solid darkness. No demons. But I couldn't see the bottom, either.

I kept an eye on Martin, waiting for the right moment to drop the gun. But he was too close—he'd see me.

He rooted through the dirt at our feet and handed me a rock.

"See if you can hear it hit bottom."

I took the stone, dropped it in, and leaned forward to listen to it plummet. It made no sound.

On our way back up, I heard the rev of a motorcycle. A red four-wheeler cut across the path with the force of a buffalo pursued by lions. A boy maybe sixteen years old, with a buzz haircut and dressed all in black, clutched the handlebars and stood halfway up as he rode, like a racehorse jockey. Reese Witherspoon had by this point abandoned us and now trotted behind him.

"Kid's a handful," Martin said.

He stopped me before I walked back to my car.

"You need a place to sleep tonight, Father? Where you staying?"

I told him I'd been planning to camp somewhere, but he insisted on hosting me. I was ready to cave. It was getting dark, and I was tired. Sleeping in my car was starting to take its toll. The muscles in my back were so tight you could have played me like a harp. I could barely turn my head. I agreed to stay the night, and he led me into the house.

"I was raised Catholic," he told me after he sat me on the couch and handed me a beer. He still went to Mass every now and then. His wife had been the organist at the local parish before she died, about five years ago. I offered my condolences, and he gave a quick nod. They had someone else playing now, who wasn't nearly as good as his wife had been, little better than one of those keyboard-playing cats on YouTube, really, and this affirmation of his wife's talent comforted him, was probably the main reason he ever went to Mass anymore, to see other people forced to reckon with the vacuum left by her gift.

He pointed out the organ in a corner of the room. I'd noticed it right away. With its tall cabinet of knobs and keys, it had the complexity of a Jain shrine, or a pinball machine.

"My daughter, Anna, still plays," he said. "I'll make her play something for us after dinner. I think she's cooking right now."

A few minutes later, the boy from the four-wheeler appeared.

"Dinner's ready."

Martin's daughter.

We sat at the dining-room table and ate chili from a slow cooker.

"You ever been to Kansas before, Padre?"

"Not really. Just a little while when I was a kid. I grew up in Indiana."

"Oh, I'm sorry. At least it wasn't Oklahoma. If you fall into the pit, you wind up about four miles outside of Tulsa."

Reese Witherspoon rested against my foot. He

wheezed loudly, and his tail kept drumming against the leg of the chair. The gun was still tucked into the pocket of my jacket—I reached inside to make sure it was secure.

"You know about the pope in Topeka?" Martin asked.

I told him I had no idea.

"It might've been Belvue, actually. Some guy got together with his mom and declared himself pope. Pope Michael, I think. I don't remember names. He thinks he's the true pope and everyone else after the Vatican Council is an impostor. It's a good idea. I'd keep my name, though. First thing I would do as pope is let you guys marry. It would solve some of the weird shit you've all been up to. Not you—you know what I mean. But even for you good ones, it's got to be lonely for you guys."

"It's not too bad."

"I'll make you a cardinal. I hope you like red."

"Anything else I should see around here? Now that I've checked the pit off my list."

"Hmm. You ever been to Coronado's Castle?"

"I haven't."

"Coronado was this Spanish explorer."

"He was an asshole," Anna said.

"They found some chain mail outside of Lindsborg. This was in the twenties. After a while they built this castle on a hill. You can go up in there. It's pretty neat."

"It's fake," Anna said.

"I'm a history buff," Martin continued. "Sometimes I wish our country had more history, just so I could know it. I'd like to write a book about BTK. That's bind-torture-kill. He was from Wichita. His daughter went to K-State, like I did. Father, you like history?"

I told him I did. "Mostly medieval stuff."

"Oh wow. Wait a minute. You're going to love this."

He disappeared, and Anna and I sat there in silence. On the wall behind her hung a picture of her standing next to a seal or a sea lion. She had long black hair, the color of the seal.

She caught me looking.

"I used to have such good hair. I'm not bragging— I'm quoting my mom. I'm going to grow it back out."

"Why'd you cut it?"

"My dad makes me shave it every couple weeks because I set it on fire twice. Three times. It's fun to do, but it smells awful."

Martin returned, carrying what appeared to be an enormous ax.

"One of my friends trades in these things, and I've been buying off him every now and then since Carla died."

"Of lupus," Anna said.

"This is a halberd. A poleax. The Swiss were all about these guys in the fifteen-hundreds. You used them against the cavalry. Swing it like a kaiser blade. Kind of like this."

"You're poking the wallpaper," Anna said.

"You try, Father."

People like to show priests their oddities, their religious baubles, their own personal relics, the same way they like to talk about their miracles. I've been shown vials of holy water from Lourdes and the River Jordan, innumerable decks of holy cards, galleries' worth of bad paintings of Jesus, countless urns, and, during a trip I took to Israel with Paul in the nineties, the arm of a saint, encased in silver. It was the size of a baby's arm, but its owner was still convinced it was authentic.

I took the weapon and examined the blade, which was shaped like a butterfly's wing. Anna and Martin were reflected in it, warped in the metal so that their heads looked like one cell, some pink amoeba dividing. Staring into the steel, I wondered if I might hand the bone gun off to Martin. My Montana fantasy was starting to seem more and more absurd the longer I was around other people. I could find another way to make up for what I did and didn't do. And Martin might like the thing. He could keep it in his garage arsenal with his halberd.

But if I were to get rid of it, I thought, I'd do better simply to bless the bone and toss it into the pit. I decided I'd try to sneak down there later, after I checked up on the coyote.

I shifted the blade in my hands, and that was when the dog rushed out and began jumping up, barking at me and baring his butter-colored teeth.

I gave the ax back to Martin, and Anna yelled at the dog until he ran away.

"Anna!" Martin shouted once we were settled back in the living room.

"What?"

"Play something for Father . . . Father . . . I'm sorry. What's your first name?"

"Dan. You can just call me Dan."

"Play something for Father Dan."

"I practiced all afternoon. My fingers hurt."

Martin got up and flipped the switch on the back of the organ. Then, after theatrically stretching out his fingers like a maestro, he began pounding the keys in short, angry bursts, moaning along to the music in some other key.

It didn't take long for Anna to get sick of this and push him aside. She washed out our ears with a few gurgling arpeggios and then began a proper song.

I regret to say it, but Catholics have been terrible at music for at least 120 years, probably longer. In my opinion, the peak of Catholic liturgical music is to be found in the choral works of the Renaissance. Sometime since, we've stopped caring about it, and in my lifetime I've had to endure a cycle of somnolent organists, sad John Denver clones, and terrible Billy Joel rip-offs. I'm not disposed to liking the organ, is what I'm saying.

But the music the girl played was some other thing. Like a horror-movie score, but with some sweetness mixed in. The room filled up with it, so that the whole house hummed and twitched with the sadness it carried. It reached into me and wrapped its spidery legs around my stomach. I was inside the envelope in my cup holder, in the middle of a mountain of birds. It squeezed me through the center of a giant pewter ring. I couldn't hide my reaction—at one point, Martin even shot me a concerned look. I considered getting up to use the bathroom to escape, but I didn't want to be rude. When it was over, the last note hung in the air for a while, until it was finally absorbed into the walls and floorboards.

In the middle of the night, I snuck out of the house, careful to guide the door into its frame to keep things quiet.

The coyote seemed fine. I gave him some more Spam and another pill, along with a refill of water. The car smelled like salt-and-vinegar potato chips, though I'd never eaten those in there. I took his soiled blanket and tossed it on one of the rusty pieces of farm equipment in the grass.

As I locked up the Camry, I saw light down below,

by the pit. A spray of blue fire. A spirit, it looked like, bursting forth from the underworld.

I took the gun with me, stuck into the inside pocket of my denim jacket, and followed the light down the hill. The long bone ran along my ribs like the beginning of a strange exoskeleton.

About halfway down, I nearly bumped into something on the path. The dog, sitting in his usual spot, keeping watch over the fields and pit below.

The sky was a living veil. The moon was full, or mostly full, and the stars seemed to multiply when I looked up at them, like bacteria spawning in the heat of my breath. By the time I got close to the pit, I could make out the outlines of three people—Anna and two others.

Anna took something from the pocket of her hoodie and lit a cigarette lighter. Fire sprayed from her, and the hole glowed with a swirl of blue light.

"*Ad astra per aspera, motherfucker!*"

One of the others saw me in the glow.

"Holy shit!" they shouted, and I stepped closer so all of them could see me.

"What the fuck are you doing down here?" Anna asked.

I told them I'd gone out to my car and saw the blue light and wanted to see what it was.

"I thought you were a murderer."

One of the boys (the other two appeared to be boys) was tall, well over six feet, and wore a blue sweatshirt with the hood pulled up. He was the first black person I'd seen since I passed Kansas City. The other boy was short, with long, girlish hair.

"You're a priest," the tall one said.

"Yep."

"Priests are scary," the short boy said.

The tall boy: "Do you believe in God the Father Almighty, Creator of Heaven and Earth? And in Jesus-Christ-His-only-begotten-Son-our-Lord?"

"Stop," Anna said. The tall boy, she told me, was named Andre. The one with the long hair was Pete.

"Want a beer?" Anna asked, and handed me a tall can of Pabst Blue Ribbon.

I wanted to show them that I could be trusted, that I wasn't some rigid, adult tattle or old-school Eisenhower priest. So I took the beer.

They studied me as I opened the can and took a sip.

Anna handed me a blue rocket and her lighter.

"Just shoot it down into the hole."

I aimed the rocket and, after flicking the lighter a few times, lit the fuse. The light sprayed forth and the rocket careened into the pit, filling it with blue light. I tried to track it as it flew down, but somewhere along the way it bumped into the tunnel, turned a corner, and vanished.

By drinking the beer and lighting the rocket, it

seemed I'd more or less been initiated into their teenage ritual, or at least made myself sufficiently complicit to keep from ratting on them, like a dirty cop.

"Where are you going?" Anna asked. "Don't you have a church?"

"Not really. I'm retired. Going to see some friends in Seattle."

Anna: "I've always wanted to go there. I've never even seen the ocean. I've seen the Gulf of Mexico, but I don't think it counts."

Pete: "It counts. It's contiguous with the ocean. It's the ocean."

Andre: "Father, you've caught us at a bad time. We were just gonna do 'shrooms."

"I'm already doing them." Pete gave us a maniac grin. "Just a tiny amount."

"I need a food taster for my drugs," Andre said. "Like the kings of yore."

"You guys need to shut the fuck up," Anna said. "He's a priest."

I still felt like I had to prove myself, so I told them about how Paul and I used to get high in seminary. I kept it short this time.

"That would freak me out," Andre said. "All the statues."

Anna looked at me as if I'd audibly farted. "We mostly just do Roman candles and microdose."

She took the lighter back and flicked it a few times.

"This one's dead."

"There's another in the truck."

The boy with the long hair tossed her the keys.

"She's a fucking pyro," Andre said once Anna was out of earshot. Up close, I saw he had a gold nose ring. "Martin tell you about the Pizza Hut?"

I told him I didn't know anything about that.

"Oh man. Last year, she burned down a Pizza Hut and they sent her to a school for fucked-up girls in Salina. I was there when she lit it up. She started with some pizza boxes, and the rest of it burned on its own from there. Pretty efficient, from a physics point of view."

Anna came back with the lighter. I could see the flame in the darkness, flickering into existence, going out again.

"I was just telling Father about how you're a pyro."

"Fuck you."

She lit another rocket and shot it down.

I tried to defuse things.

"How deep you think it goes?"

"China," Andre said.

"I think it's about as deep as a well," Anna said. "I don't believe in Hell."

She turned to Andre.

"Isn't it your bedtime? Don't you have work in the morning?"

"I don't sleep. You know I never sleep."

Andre worked for a cleaning service, he said, mostly night shifts, but also the occasional fill-in in the mornings, which was what he was doing tomorrow.

"I like working nights. I'm an insomniac." He said this proudly. "We clean the same rotation of businesses around Salina. A small IT company four nights a week, and a bariatric clinic, a clinic where they study fat people so they can make them less . . . less . . . I guess just make them less. You find crazy shit in people's trash," he added.

"Like what?" I asked.

"People think things are gone forever once they throw them away, but, like, they're still right there. One time, I found a dead guinea pig in an office trash can. It was all stiff and crunchy, and its eyes were open. I found a pair of white pants covered in drops of blood. I found a Ziploc bag *packed* with toenails. Maybe fingernails in there, too, but there were definitely toenails, because nobody has fingers that big. Some of these were like croissants."

One night, he was cleaning one of the offices when he saw a chessboard, on a small table in the corner. After vacuuming the carpet and emptying the trash (which they did every night in every bin, even if the trash bags had plenty of room, with just a disposable coffee cup or a ball of paper at the bottom), he came back to the board and—on a whim—moved one of the pieces forward. A white pawn, of course, because white always moves first, a rule probably laid down by the racist kings who invented the game in the days of yore. He moved the piece its permitted two spaces, thus beginning the King's Indian Attack, or the Barcza System (his dad was a chess head who had imparted to him the game's basic strategies and terminology when he was little), and as soon as he set the piece down forgot all about it. He cleaned the next office, and the next, and then drove home. But the next night, when he returned, he saw that his move had been countered, with a black pawn to e6. So he countered with a white pawn to d3 and left.

"It kept happening like that, turn by turn. I would spend my whole shift, sometimes the whole day, figuring out my next move, and then I would execute it. For two weeks we played, two moves per day, in what was, by any standard, a very tough game. Still the hardest game I've played in my life, of any kind of game."

He said he scanned the employee's office, looking for clues as to what kind of person he was, and therefore what kind of player he might turn out to be. Aggressive? Defensive? Sneaky? The man had a photo of a child on his desk, a young boy, but none of a wife, no full family portraits, and so he thought he might be divorced. His bookshelf, instead of featuring the standard Dale Carnegie books, had novels (Philip K. Dick, some Russians and French guys) and at least one book of photography. For bookends he had two statues of Bart Simpson. These details didn't offer much insight into the man's overall strategy, but did endear the stranger to his opponent.

"It was like he was a ghost. A friendly ghost. Or maybe it was more like I was a ghost, since it was his office and I only came out at night. I didn't know him, but I liked him. It was like a friendship, but without the guilt and mind games. Just a game-game, you know?"

A few rounds in, he told his dad about it, since he knew the man would be interested. Because the game had been so slow, and because he'd had so much time to think about each move, he could recall the rounds with perfect clarity, illustrating the game on the board in his father's basement.

"And my dad was like, 'Holy shit! It's Fischer-Myagmarsuren!' We had, he said, perfectly re-created a game between Bobby Fischer and some Mongolian guy. Which meant that, if I studied the game, I might beat him, as long as he didn't veer from the Mongolian master's moves. My dad showed me a website that walked you through the game—through every game ever played, what they call 'The Book'—and I took notes. I vowed to defeat him. To smite my invisible foe and cast his remains into the sea, so to speak. But we never finished. After my next move, the board was reset. Maybe the stranger realized what was happening. Or maybe his kid had come to the office and fucked with the pieces to the point where he couldn't remember what was what. Maybe I had messed up the vibe by consulting my dad, or the guy didn't want to be defeated by a janitor, I don't know. I would have won, though. I was going to kick his ass. I really was going to vanquish him. That's the weirdest thing that's happened at that job, I guess. Along with tidying up the oversized bariatric equipment."

"Why didn't you reset the pieces?" Pete asked. "If you remembered the game?"

"I tried that, actually. He didn't pick it back up. We lost something, the flow."

While he spoke, I waited for the right moment to drop the gun. But all three of them were staring right into the hole. There was no way for me to mumble my blessing and toss it down without looking very strange. I could only watch and wait.

"Can we talk about something else?" Anna said. "Jesus, he tells that story all the fucking time." She held the rockets by their stems and flicked them against her leg.

"Give me one of those," Andre said. He reached out, and I saw his fingernails were painted neon pink.

"No way. I'm the pyro. They're mine."

The two of them scuffled for the rockets and the lighter. As I stood there wondering just how I should intercede, Andre pried them out of Anna's hands and managed to light all the fuses at once. For a moment, all of us—even Andre—were transfixed by the bright, hissing bouquet. But as he tried to chuck it toward the pit, Anna caught his arm and he fumbled the toss. The bundle of rockets fell a couple feet shy of the hole.

"Oh fuck."

We ducked down, and everything turned blue. By the time I got up, the kids were already running off. The headlights of the truck passed over me and I watched the taillights float away.

I'd made it half the way up the hill when I saw Reese Witherspoon again. I thought of St. Guinefort, Paul's pious dog saint venerated for his protection of infants. This dog certainly comported himself with saintly Zen. Had he really fallen into the hole, like Martin said? What had he seen down there in the pit? How'd he come back from infinity?

The screen door slammed up at the house. I ran into the brush off to the side of the path. The dog turned and stared at me.

Up the hill, I spotted Martin, running with a flashlight in his hand. And something else, something glinting in the flash- and moonlight.

It was the halberd. The blade hovered above his head like an evil moth.

The air turned into pudding. I held my breath and hoped Martin wouldn't notice the dog looking at me.

He ran by with his light and his blade and stopped to regard the dog. Some of the moonlight bounced off his head as he turned toward me. But then he continued down the hill. The blade still hung above him, a big white wing in the moonlight, and I tracked its flight as Martin circled the pit and shouted into the fields. His hollering was desperate and animal, and some of the cows past the fence heard it and began to moo back at him.

I crept back into the house, and a few minutes later, I could hear Anna and Martin fighting through the walls. I did my best to ignore them and maximize my chance for rest in an actual bed. Still, sleep was hard. On the nightstand sat a tchotchke gang of ceramic fruits and vegetables with clowny eyes, white gloves, and cowboy boots dangling over the drawer. I stared at the onion for a while. He had big green teardrops painted under his eyes, and with his ample rump looked like an unhappy king.

Thanks to him, my dreams were packed with that saddest of vegetables, peeling off their translucent layers and making my dream-eyes fill with tears.

11

The next morning, I packed my things and prepared to slip out of the house with as little fuss as possible. I wasn't sure if Anna had mentioned my being down there with them or not, and I thought I might as well go before Martin had the chance to ask me about it.

I went to the kitchen to fill my water jug and found Martin, drinking a glass of orange juice. The halberd was there, too, leaning against the stove.

"I don't know what all you heard last night. Me and the girl have been having trouble lately. It's probably best if you just go."

She hadn't mentioned me.

I told him I'd seen a lot of messed-up families, and his was far from the worst. This seemed to cheer him up slightly. I was grateful the girl hadn't ratted me out, but now I can see I was being a coward. I could have been a witness for her.

I am a coward, but you probably know that already.

On the way out, I paused in front of the organ in the living room. I counted the knobs. There were twenty-six. I felt for the switch on the back and flipped it.

I pressed the highest key with my pinkie. It produced a warbly, science-fictional note, heralding an alien.

I turned off the organ and left the house.

The car still smelled awful. The salt and vinegar had given way to the stench of a shoe soaked in rain. But the coyote seemed to be doing okay. He was up on his legs as I fed him his Spam and pill. The gauze was still mostly in place, but I could see he'd ripped off big pieces from the topmost layers. I wondered if his leg was, in fact, broken as badly as I first suspected. In any case, he seemed to be making a speedy recovery.

I drove west for an hour or so, past more farms and oil derricks bobbing like drinking birds. Just shy of Hays, I spilled some of my water onto the console and, terrified it would get to the green envelope, immediately ferreted through the CDs to save it. I had nothing to worry about. Most of the spill had been soaked up by a wad of cocktail napkins and old receipts.

A billboard read "CHOOSE LIFE." It sounded like something Jesus would say, but not in the way it was meant here.

"Hey. It's me."

I was so surprised that I accelerated, sending us up to eighty or ninety miles. The rearview was a beige trapezoid with eyes.

"It smells fucking terrible in here."

Anna. She'd folded over one of the back seats and poked her head through the gap.

"You have a dog?"

"It's a coyote. It got hit by a car."

"It's been with you this whole time?"

"How'd you get in here?"

"I spent the night in the barn. I saw you getting ready to leave, so I hopped in the trunk. It was unlocked. What the fuck is this?"

I looked back. Anna had squeezed her arm through and now held the derringer by the bone.

"I'm returning it to a friend."

"Is that a real bone? I want this."

"I'm taking you back."

"I want you to drive me to Seattle."

"I can't do that."

"I demand sanctuary."

"It doesn't work that way."

"Why not?"

"You're not a refugee. You're a teenager. This isn't a church. It's a car."

The coyote grunted inside the carrier. I had the impression he was complaining about all the noise we were making.

"Can you pull over so I can at least get in the front?

It's cramped back here. And it smells like literal shit. I need some air or it's going to start smelling like puke, too."

I pulled over to the shoulder, and she got in the passenger seat. She'd brought a fat black backpack with her, which she wedged into the footwell. "I'm taking you home."

"I don't want to go back. You can leave me wherever, but you are not taking me back. I'll hitchhike or something. You can take me with you or leave me here."

She opened the door, grabbed her backpack as she swung back out, and started walking along the shoulder.

A truck sped by, and I felt the car wobble in its draft.

I couldn't leave her there. I pulled up behind her before she got too far, and told her to get in.

Anna knew she'd won. She sat down and celebrated her victory by eating a rope of red licorice she pulled out of her bag, whipping it against the dash once, then twice, before biting off the end. She let the rest hang out of her mouth like the tongue of a parched lizard.

"Want one?"

She handed me a piece and turned up the radio. I got back onto the interstate, keeping my eyes open for a good place to stop and figure out how to fix this.

The billboard read "WORLD'S LARGEST BALL OF PAINT NEXT EXIT." Under the words was painted a plain blue circle, which I assumed was supposed to represent the ball of paint, being a ball of paint itself. When the next exit came, I took it.

The ball was kept in a giant barn visible right off the exit. Like Martin and Anna's, this one doubled as a billboard, with its roof painted with the words:

WORLD'S LARGEST BALL OF PAINT
BROUGHT TO YOU
BY SHERWIN-WILLIAMS

"What is a ball of paint?" Anna asked. "Like, for a paintball gun?"

"I don't know."

I parked the car by the barn's tin silo, and the two of us got out. The gate was locked. Anna ran around back, but the door she found was locked, too.

"I guess we'll never know," she said. "I'll look it up later."

Besides the barn, the only other buildings were a gas station and a bar.

"Think they serve food?" Anna asked.

"Let's see."

The bar was called El Greco's. The sign had been made to look like an artist's signature at the bottom of a painting, done in black, sludgy strokes. Before we went in, I took the dog carrier out of the car to air it out and fed the coyote another half-pill buried in Spam. While I spooned the clumps of meat through the grate, a man of considerable size stepped out of the bar. He wore a tight, plaid pajama shirt that made him look more upholstered than dressed. Tucked under one of his arms was a small white dog with a spiked collar.

I lifted the carrier back into the car.

"No, no. Bring him on in. We're pro-dog here. Dog-friendly."

Anna looked to me, and, fearing the man would escalate things, I carried the coyote into the bar.

Inside, the walls were covered in poster copies of famous paintings. Fat van Gogh sunflowers. Dalí's dripping clocks. Rembrandt in his white hat, standing in front of two semicircles. There was a pinball machine in the corner, and Anna went straight to it.

"Sit here," the man said, gesturing to a booth near the bar. He had already filled a water dish for the coyote, which he set in front of the wire door.

"Does he have any dietary restrictions?" he asked as he pulled a treat from his pocket.

"He's real sick," I explained. "It's making him a little grouchy. I don't want him biting yours. Probably best to keep him in the crate."

"He a Shiba Inu? Cattle dog? What's his name?"

"Bede."

"Like on a necklace?"

"Yeah."

"So you two come for the ball?" he asked as he handed us each a menu. "You and your . . ."

"My niece. Yeah, we wanted to see the ball."

"It was all locked up," Anna shouted across the room.

"It's pretty cool," he told us. "The first time I saw it, I couldn't believe it, but, you know, it wears off. Here, I'll show you something even more amazing. Watch this."

He poured some water into a shot glass and set it on the bar. Anna walked over.

"Sophia," he said, "time for a shot."

The white dog leapt onto the stool and, once she'd secured her footing, stood so her front legs rested on the bar. Bending over, she began to lap the water from the shot glass.

"Prost!"

"Wow," Anna said, and sat down in the booth. "Aren't you worried she'll drink whiskey or vodka or something and die?"

"She's trained," he said with some agitation. "She only does it on command. You guys know what you want?"

"I'll have a Coors Light, and a hamburger, no onions," Anna said.

"Uh-huh. And you, Padre?"

"I'll do a grilled cheese with fries. And a water, whenever it's convenient."

The man retreated to the kitchen. His dog went over to the carrier, sniffed it, and then darted away.

I considered my options. I didn't think I could persuade Anna to go back. I thought I might try to trick her, just drive toward her house under the illusion we were still headed west. But she was too smart; she'd recognize the landmarks of her childhood, the road signs, the names of towns. I wondered if I could give her another couple dollars to play pinball and use the distraction to call her father, let him know where she was.

Or I could simply take her to Seattle with me.

But of course there was no way to do this. It would amount to kidnapping. It would look terrible—a Catholic priest abducting a teenage girl. And even if we got there, I couldn't just let her loose on the streets without making sure she had someplace safe to go. It was an idiotic thought. Still, just because she was young, it didn't mean she was wrong. I admired her toughness, her ability to drop everything and leave, to keep from turning her back to the plow, so to speak.

"I have to take you home."

"I'm not going back. Did Dre or Pete tell you about when I was sent away?"

"One of them mentioned something about it. The Pizza Hut."

"It was closed. They closed for business, like, six months before that. There wasn't anybody in it. I bet they didn't tell you that. I just went in, and all the boxes were lying on the floor. I found some olive oil and poured it on those and got out of there. A few minutes later, the smoke was coming out the windows." She'd been picking a scab on her wrist and now leaned over to lap up a little garnet of blood. "Maybe I was possessed. Do you think people can be possessed by demons?"

"I've never seen a possessed person. I'm not sure it works that way. I think demons are more complicated than that. I don't know."

"I think I'm just saying that 'cause you're here. At the time, I was just kind of dazed and numb, and then, all of a sudden, I was lighting things on fire."

After the Pizza Hut, she explained, the sheriff came over and talked to her father. Together they decided to send her away to the school in Salina. A school for girls with problems. Her mother never would have let him send her there, and she told him so, but he didn't care. She came back after a year there, on the condition that if she fucked up again he was going to send her back. And last night he said she'd fucked up again.

We both became hypnotized by a margarita maker behind the bar. We watched the green vortex of margarita through its frosty, pustulated skin.

"It's not that the school was too bad. The girls were pretty nice to me. They liked me because I played the piano. They would tell me a song and I would play it for

them. Or I would figure out how if they sang me some of
it. It wasn't too bad. It just wasn't good. Like, why should
I even try to stay in a family with him if he's just going
to send me away every time he thinks I've fucked up?"

She said she'd met a girl at the school who'd hitch-
hiked all the way to Oakland, California. She could live
like that, too. She could hitchhike her way out to San
Francisco or Seattle. She would need a knife and probably a tent. A guitar would be good, too, to make money.
She should have stolen a few things from her dad before
she left, but she was in too much of a hurry.

"He has a dagger that would be perfect."

Anna took the ashtray in the middle of the table and
cupped it in her hands. She stared down into it like it was
another bottomless pit.

"I knew this girl from the school who put out cigarettes on her arm. She put them out on her arms and
hands and never flinched or made a sound. They gave
her spots that looked like chewed-up gum. She didn't
even smoke much, but just took someone else's cigarette
and put it out. She was running out of space."

"There's no way they let you smoke."

"We weren't supposed to have cigarettes, but sometimes we could get people to bring them to us. We could
get all kinds of things. There was a chain-link fence
around the school, and someone could just drop things
through that. One of my bunkmates' sisters lived in

Salina, where the school was, and she would drop mini-bar bottles through the hexagons. Those teeny bottles from hotels." She ran her fingers back and forth over her buzz, as if her thoughts were surfacing to her scalp in Braille. "We reused them all the time, just took the labels off and filled them up with juice and shampoo. A girl I shared a room with had a boyfriend we'd get candy and most of the cigarettes from. He wrote her long letters, and we passed them around at night. She broke up with him, and then someone else at the school started dating him. I thought that was weird, that they would start dating while she was in there, but someone told me that that was how it was with the first girl, too. She'd inherited him from someone else in the school who'd broken up with him. It was his thing, I guess."

She started looking at my head. "Hey, are you okay?"

I'd begun to sweat. My face felt like a wet balloon. I'd been trying to listen as best I could, but the problem of what to do with Anna was getting to me. Was Martin safe for her to live with, running around with his battle-ax? Probably not. But it wasn't my responsibility to decide that. Or was it?

"Anyway, the letters were bad, but in a sweet way. My dad didn't even write me one letter."

"He cares a lot about you," I said. "I think that's why he got so angry."

I don't know why I was siding with her father, and regretted saying this immediately.

"He's forbidden me to see those guys, even though I'm more of an influence on them than the other way around. I make them come down there all the time. I like to hang out there. My mother is down there."

"What? She's buried there?" I imagined her body down there, illuminated by the occasional firework or odd cigarette butt.

"Oh, fuck no. Not literally. I just like to go and pretend she and my grandpa are down there, and if I hang out I can be close to them. Let them know I'm there. My grandpa liked fireworks, too."

The man appeared with the food and Anna's beer. He hadn't asked her for an ID. I wasn't sure if he was gullible or if he just didn't care.

"You know why we call this place El Greco's?" he asked as he set the plates on the table.

"Because of the painter," Anna said. "And the ball of paint."

"Yes, exactly. I like you." He put the can of Coors in front of her.

I liked Anna, too. Why should she go back to her father? I still wouldn't take her to Seattle, but I understood her anger. My father had been the county coroner. He was also a drunk. He would get drunk and rant about being a coroner. He told us stories about his work like he was telling jokes, all with the same sour punch line. One about a man who cut off his own foot with a chain saw. One about a woman who lunged into the blades of a combine. One about two guys who played Russian roulette with a semi-automatic pistol. This one he acted out using a banana. He cocked the banana and held it up to the side of his head, pulled its invisible trigger and flopped onto the floor. When I tried to leave the room, he aimed the banana at my head and told me to sit down or he'd shoot me. I was seven.

The proprietor played an ABBA song on a boom box in the kitchen.

Anna pointed to her throat.

"You've got some ketchup on your collar."

I pulled it out and dabbed it with the napkin.

"Can I touch it?"

"Sure."

I pulled out the white boomerang of my collar. She stuck it on her neck, then put it as a mustache under her nose.

"I used to want to be a priest. My mom said I couldn't, so I settled on nun. I like the costume. The habit. Living all-women. That could be cool. The school was like that, and I liked it. But I don't think I'm meant for it. I never really heard 'the Calling.' When did you hear yours?"

"It's not that interesting."

"I'm sure it can't be that boring."

"There's not much to it."

Anna downed her beer and water and began to eat the ice, plucking the cubes from the glass and popping them into her mouth like grapes.

"Are you sure there's no way I can go with you?"

The carrier door rattled. Some of the coyote's hairs poked through the gills on the side of the crate.

"I can take you."

It just came out of my mouth like that. But after I said it, I had no desire to take it back. Even Anna seemed startled by my answer. I wouldn't allow myself to consider the logistics or the difficulties. Instead of going to Montana, I'd leave Bruno to rot and I'd take care of Anna. I would drive her wherever she needed to go. I'd find her a place to stay where she could start a new life. I could rearrange the back of the car, put Bede in the trunk so she wouldn't have to deal with him. If I had to jump into the bottomless pit on her behalf, I was convinced I would do it.

As I settled the check at the bar, I picked up a guide to roadside attractions lying there under a trophy cup full of pens.

"You can keep that," the bartender said. "It's expired."

"Thanks."

"She your niece, you said?"

"Yeah. My brother's daughter."

"How long you been a priest?"

"About fifty years."

"Sounds hard. I bet it's good to have family."

"Really is."

I slid him my signed receipt in its black vinyl wallet.

"Thanks, Father."

People call you "Father," but you're never truly a father to anyone. It's the irony of the collar. You're called a thing you can never be, by people who come and go in your life. What's worse is that, because of the Brunos and those who protect them, people are wary of any priest who comes near children and teenagers. For good reason. But it has made things lonely. I've always wished I could have been a real father to someone. Or a mother. To make a person out of almost nothing. I wish I could have taken care of someone like Anna. It is a terrible feeling, worse than puking.

I'd tipped the cost of the meal. The man peeked into the black vinyl wallet holding the receipt, shook his head, and slid me a five-dollar bill across the counter. Anna had by this point wandered over to us and was eyeing the fishbowl full of matchboxes by the register.

"So the guy who runs the ball is out of town. He's got a place in Sarasota, Florida. He gave me the keys to look after things. If you two want to take a look, I can let you in."

"Sure!" Anna said. I picked up the carrier, and he swooped up his dog and walked us outside.

"What is a ball of paint?" Anna asked as he unlocked the doors.

"It started as a baseball," he said. "And then the guy added a layer of paint every day. This guy is actually dead, the one who started it. His kids sold it to the Florida guy. One microscopic layer every day. Over the years, it's gotten really, really thick, and there you've got your ball of paint. And this is the largest one. Might be one of the only ones, as far as I know. Not my ball."

The ball was the size of an armchair. It hung from an industrial hook so that the bottom dangled two or three feet above the floor. It wasn't a perfect sphere—not even close. More of an egg shape, with uneven, brain-like ridges from where the paint drifted as it dried. Its present shade was a faded coral pink, almost the color of my skin. It looked as if it might at any moment hatch and give birth to a giant, slime-covered monster with too many arms and eyes.

"I told you it wasn't much," the man said. "But there is something to it."

He stood in admiration of the thing, taking in its beauty as if gazing upon some wide river or deep canyon.

"You can paint it," he said, pointing to a pyramid of paint cans along the wall. "But you have to do a whole coat. That's the deal."

"Okay," Anna said. "What color?"

"It doesn't matter."

She picked lime green.

"All right. The rollers are right here. I gotta go take care of the place. Just lock the door behind you when you go."

Anna thanked him, and I poured some of the paint into a roller tray.

It took us almost an hour to cover the thing. The rollers, made for flat surfaces, didn't quite fit the contours of the ball, leaving only a narrow stripe of paint behind.

We developed a system. Anna applied fat globs of paint with the roller, and I tidied her work with a brush, smoothing the paint for an even coat. I found it satisfying, spreading the paint, guiding it into the ball's grooves and clefts. The coyote watched us from inside the carrier, his yellow eyes giving off rings of light like the ends of car cigarette lighters.

When we were done, it looked like a peeled avocado. Anna orbited the ball, trying to blow on every inch of paint to help it dry.

"Now we've left our mark on the world," I said.

I turned and saw Anna leaning against the wall, watching the ball spin.

"Can you take me home?"

12

The first time I met Paul, he was sitting on the bunk on top of the one assigned to me, his legs hanging over the edge, as he strummed a mint-green souvenir ukulele.

Salve, Regina, pray for this hairy horny ape.
Vita, dulcedo, and this cobra between his legs.

The ukulele had a sticker of St. Francis on it: Francis with his punctured palms and his pate looking like a lone egg in an ostrich nest.

"I'm Paul," he said. He drummed on the back of the instrument. "This is Frank."

Later, I'd learn that the sticker was a kind of talisman, meant to ward off the priests and older kids who daily threatened to take the ukulele away.

"Nice to meet you, Frank."

I reached out and shook the ukulele's neck like it was a hand.

For the next few weeks, I would be the 3D version of the St. Francis sticker, cloaking Paul from the stricter priests with my quiet obedience, until my association with him was widely known and the immunity wore off. By then it didn't matter—I was his friend.

After a month, he told me he had something he wanted to show me and led me to the auditorium. We went backstage, and I followed him up a ladder to a loft full of balled-up curtains and rugs rolled as tight as joints. An apt simile, given what he was about to pull out from behind them.

"I keep some things up here," he said. "Odds and ends. They don't really do plays or musicals anymore, so no one's ever up here."

He reached into a shoe box and produced a plastic bag with a dry bulb of weed and a lonely, skinny joint in it, along with a box of matches as long as pencils. He struck one of the matches on the floor, looking like a magician conjuring fire with his wand. We smoked for a minute as I looked through the box of things he'd holed away up there: a Playboy magazine from 1959 he'd stolen from an uncle (the cover showed a woman and an anthropomorphic rabbit riding mopeds), a small flask of bourbon, and a cube of red plastic with a baby scorpion suspended inside.

"Prepare yourself for the greatest of my treasures."

Paul reached behind a pile of curtains and produced a large bowl, which he set on the ground and plugged in.

The bowl lit up green, revealing a statuette of Mary perched on an island in the middle with a halo of wires radiating from her head and to the edge of the bowl.

"Give it a few seconds."

Beads of wax began to drip from her head, then ran down the wires and melted back into a reservoir under the Virgin's sandals.

"Mary, Queen of Snots," he said.

We sang his bad Salve Regina parody as the glowing beads of slime crawled along the strings. I didn't have anything against the Virgin Mother. But I wanted Paul to like me. Mary would understand.

Paul, I'd gradually learn, hadn't always been this way. There was a time, a few of the older boys told me, when he was among the top of the class. There weren't many relics from Paul's days of piety, with the exception of a few old grudges. The biggest was against Bruno, who was more than ten years older than us and already ordained at that point. Bruno was something of a star at John Bosco's. His theology courses were incredibly popular, a fact that had more to do with his secular credentials than his readings of Augustine or Bernard of Clairvaux. He'd been tight end for Notre Dame (Indiana's Vatican, if not America's) before he'd heard his calling, and could play all the Paul Butterfield solos and Lightnin' Hopkins licks on his Fender Stratocaster with perfect fluency. On Friday and Saturday nights, you could hear him practice through the walls, with his posse in tow. This was all allowed by the senior faculty because his theology was ultra-orthodox. He made Martin of Tours look like Martin Luther. He kept a painting of John Calvin on his wall, and on the last day of his class, students were encouraged to deface the heretic's likeness with permanent markers and red paint from the art room. I myself, with my artistic knack, had given the Frenchman a fairly naturalistic Hitler mustache on top of his gray beard, a graffito to which I attribute my A-minus in Bruno's Aquinas course.

Bruno's protégés were among the more popular boys in school, and it was an open secret that he supplied them with cigarettes, whiskey, and weed. From what I gathered, Paul had been one of his favorites before I'd arrived, though there'd been some falling-out. Paul especially hated Bruno, and avoided him whenever he could. Even other priests tolerated this avoidance—Paul was, for reasons unknown to me at the time, permitted to skip Bruno's required theology classes and instead use the period as a study hall. He never said anything about it to me, and I didn't ask. I knew there was some dark room inside him that was locked away from me, but at the time I simply thought it had to do with his parents' deaths, another piece of my friend's history I had to learn about secondhand.

For one reason or another, Paul was good friends with the groundskeeper, an older man who, in addition to trimming the minor seminary's lawns, also kept up on the repairs and plumbing, waxed the floors, and even occasionally worked in the kitchen, where he cooked up pink tomatoes and infant-sized squash from his garden. Paul said he'd heard that this man had fought in the Pacific Theater. His arms were covered in deep, wormy grooves, like driftwood. He had a large collection of jazz records we heard playing in his shed: Sidney Bechet, Count Basie, Lester Young, along with a bunch of novelty recordings, silly joke songs with strange gimmicks, songs about flying saucers and dancing swamp creatures.

Paul's parents had died when he was ten, and his remaining family lived in California. For the winter holidays, he stayed at school under the watch of the groundskeeper, and, my second year, I decided I'd keep him company. Through some turn of events that was never revealed to me, Paul had another friend, a boy in Indianapolis, who supplied him with pot, and that Christmas he visited, showing up on a powder-blue motorcycle. He had long red hair and wore enormous sunglasses. He at once reminded me of Art Garfunkel and someone who would happily beat the shit out of Art Garfunkel.

He'd come, Paul explained, to take mushrooms on the grounds.

"I want to do it with all the statues and old shit around," the red-haired boy said in the pseudo-accent of people from the state's southernmost toe. Paul intended to do it, too, and I was welcome to try.

The boy rode us around on his motorcycle (it was

an unseasonably warm December, one that felt like fall).
Paul and I took turns riding on the back. His orange
curls kept getting in my face, but his hair smelled good.
When I asked him about it, he told me he used a special
oil from a mail-order catalogue and promised to write
down the name of it for me later.

Paul and the kid scouted out a spot: the sunken garden, a man-made gorge dug near the woods on the edge
of the seminary grounds where one could venerate the
mysteries of Jesus's life among tarnished statues, half-
dead rosebushes, and the occasional crushed beer can
left by other delinquent students. This holy trench gave
us perfect cover. We'd be far enough from the eye of the
groundskeeper while still surrounded by the necessary
iconography that was, according to the red-haired kid,
absolutely essential to the enterprise. And if we saw the
groundskeeper approaching, we could always vanish
into the woods just ten yards away.

We set up camp, pinning down a picnic blanket
with a couple thermoses of water. From the pockets of
his bomber jacket the red-haired boy removed a plastic
bag full of mushrooms, which he ground up in a tiny
mortar and pestle before mixing it with water in the biggest thermos cap. Before we drank, though, Paul pulled
something from his bag: a chalice.

"Don't worry," he said to me. "It's a new one. It
hasn't been used in a Mass yet. No blood, no foul."

He poured the sludgy concoction into the goblet, and one by one we drank of it.

We set the chalice in the grass and sat there for a while. Paul had brought his ukulele and strummed a few verses of "Don't Let Me Be Misunderstood." The red-haired boy stared at a relief of the Agony in the Garden, and soon I found myself staring into it, too. Look, he said. Look. Suddenly Christ was moving. So were His apostles, breathing as they slept in a dog pile behind their kneeling Lord. The bloodied sweat on Christ's brow ran down His face like raindrops on a windshield.

The garden itself began to breathe around us, to pulsate and contract like the drumhead of a giant jellyfish. Each of us got lost in his own sensory bewilderments. It was not completely unlike the wobbly auras of my migraines, but without the ensuing headache.

Somewhere in my increasingly geometrical visions, I saw Paul shaking and shivering, with his back against one of the mysteries. He started crying, but when I reached out to him, he jerked away and curled into a ball, and I got lost in the undulating grass.

Eventually, we returned to one another from our respective cosmoi. Still high, but more aware and in control now. It was decided that we should venture into the compound. The sun was setting. We'd been out there for four hours already.

We got up, and as we turned back to the buildings, the red-haired boy stepped on Paul's ukulele, making a strange, incredibly loud chord that hung in the air for minutes, like colored smoke. Paul studied the mangled pieces of the instrument for a while and then led us to the chapel.

By now, our complete separateness had fizzled off entirely, and we had become a giant six-legged creature of a single will, lurking the ambulatory, lighting the candles. We chattered in the dark. We hummed songs, we ran up and down the aisle. We took off our shirts and pants, reveling in our wildness. We were silent, and then we were talking over one another, caught in dumb tangles of language. We ran into the sacristy and took the chrism oil and ran it through our hair, styling it like Ricky Nelson and James Dean. The ceiling, covered with flabby angels, seemed to be as deep as the sky itself. Together we lay out on the cool stone of the nave, staring up into the high depths of the artificial heavens.

Out of nowhere, Paul produced Mary, Queen of Snots. He must have had it all along, but I hadn't noticed it until Paul plugged her in and her green rays danced on the floor.

"I don't think I'm going to go through with it," Paul told us.

"With what?" I asked, but if Paul answered, I can't

remember. I'd become wholly absorbed by the Queen's slimy radiance.

I stared at Our Lady of Mucus for a while and traced her light along the walls. I imagined we were floating up with it, into and past the ceiling, flung high above the chapel, the seminary, over the fields and highways of Indiana, the neighborhoods, parking lots, and stirring waters of the world. To the altitude where up turns to out, out to where stars, solar systems, galaxies are little more than punctuation marks, white glyphs on a black page. Through all the levels of bodily objects the three of us rose, carried on the Queen's slime-green beams, to the very edge of the universe, that final border where all of everything rushes out to nothing at precisely the speed of light.

Then, with a sigh, we were back. And right after that, the door opened.

The groundskeeper.

He saw us lying naked on the floor of the church. He stood there for a moment, ran his fingers over the treads on the opposite arm, and then shut the door. He was gone.

The three of us put our clothes back on and blew out the candles. We found a bag of unconsecrated hosts in the sacristy and ate them in the dormitory, terrified that at any moment the groundskeeper would burst in.

But he never came. In the morning, we went back out into the garden to retrieve the thermos, blanket, and chalice. Sometime in the night, the ukulele's remains had vanished. Paul figured some musical raccoon had dragged them off.

As we walked out, we passed the groundskeeper raking up dead leaves near the cloister. He said hi, and made no mention of the night before.

With the garden tidied, we snuck off to the woods to smoke a recuperative joint.

"It looked like you went to a pretty dark place back there," I told Paul. "Are you okay?"

"That's actually very common," the red-haired boy said as he pulled out his rolling papers. Paul nodded.

The red-haired boy rode away not long after, his hair Garfunkeling out from under his helmet and jiggling in the wind. From then on, he'd stop by once a month, attend a Mass as a prospective seminarian, and drop off a bag of weed as big as his head.

As for the groundskeeper, I don't know what he thought or saw. Had he actually seen us? Did we see him? Did he know what we had been up to?

Once everyone returned from vacation, we waited to be summoned to the office, but the call never came. A few days later, Paul found me in the dormitory with the green ukulele in his hand. It had appeared on his bed that afternoon. Aside from a few lacquered cracks, it was completely restored. He strummed a few bright chords as he walked it back to his bunk.

Paul dropped out the next year. I came back from a visit to my parents and learned he'd gone. I was told he'd moved to Hawaii.

Twelve years later, after I'd finished up at the major seminary and been ordained and sent to Muncie, I received a call from him. He'd gone through with it after all, and had been sent to a church in Bloomington, only two hours away.

"Do you still have that ukulele?" I asked. "Frank?"

"No, I got rid of that when I left Indiana," he told me. "I think I burned it. I didn't hang on to anything from that time."

"RIP, Frank."

Two days later, we met up at a Mexican restaurant halfway between our parishes, where he handed me his copy of Merton's *The Wisdom of the Desert*. I still have it— I put it in the trunk, so the coyote can't get to it.

13

Martin stood by the barn, painting over the graffiti that had turned "pit" into "bitch." The new paint was much too bright, leaving a giant smear of Band-Aid pink over the red. When we got closer, he threw his roller into the grass and kicked over his tray of paint.

Anna and I got out. I knew how it looked. I had to explain things right away.

"She hid in my car. I didn't know she was there until I was about an hour away."

I could tell he was about to yell at us. Anna also looked ready to punch someone, but that was her default. The three of us stood there for a moment, locked in place. Reese Witherspoon ran to the middle of our triangle and, after juking back and forth between Martin and Anna, vomited up a clump of wet grass at my feet.

Before her father could say anything, Anna ran up to him and gave him a hug. Martin's ears filled up with blood, and he started sobbing pathetically, shaking like a phone on vibrate. Anna was much more collected. She had the stern expression of a mother consoling her child. It was a weird, inverted pietà. The back of Martin's leg was covered in splashes of pink.

"Okay," Anna said, pulling away. "I need to use the bathroom."

Martin stayed outside.

I had to say something.

"She was a stowaway, I swear. We stopped once I found her. We had a pretty good talk—I was able to convince her to come home."

Nothing.

"I think she's still hurt by your sending her away to that school. She needs to know you love her."

"Thanks for the parenting advice, Father." His ears were ever redder. "Since you've raised so many kids. The Church really knows how to take care of children, huh? They teach you how to abduct teenage girls in the seminary? That in the catechism?"

I didn't have anything to say to that.

"I know you were down there last night, with the kids. What the fuck are you doing with your life?"

I turned around and got back into the car.

It was a good question.

I pulled over to the shoulder about a mile down the road and flipped through the guidebook from the restaurant. I read about a gas station in Louisiana with a white tiger in a cage. A motel in South Dakota where visitors could stay in grounded airplanes and refurbished boats. I read about a steamboat in Kansas City dug up by the family of the owner of a hamburger restaurant, an article accompanied by photos of the trove of recovered goods: a ring of old keys, Wedgwood china plates, the skull of a drowned mule that went down with the hull.

The attractions were listed by state, each given a few bland paragraphs before the site was rated on a five-star scale. I flipped to Kansas and searched for an entry on Martin's Topekan pope, but there was no sign of him or his prairie Vatican. I didn't really want an audience anyway. He was probably an asshole. Then I looked for the Hole to Hell and, to my surprise, found a brief entry buried toward the end, between two long reviews of the fake Spanish castle (the one Martin had told me about) and a giant rock shaped like a mushroom. The guide was clearly unimpressed, calling it little more than a scam and giving it just one lonely black star at the bottom of the page.

I thought about Anna and her friends gathered around this one-star wonder, about Paul at the seminary school, those boys at the parish near mine, and I recommitted myself to my plan. I reached into the pocket of my denim jacket and ran my fingers over the nubs on the derringer's bone handle like they were rosary beads.

14

I took a nap in a Kwik Shop parking lot, then drove east, to Lindsborg.

A lonely hawk sat perched on the fence wire every half-mile or so, inspecting its field or the length of road in front of it. These appeared with such consistency, on the same kind of fence, in front of the same fields, that I felt as if I was driving in a circle, lapping the same brown hawk with its speckled white chest, the same blond fields, the same fence, the same road. I had "Purple Rain" stuck in my head from karaoke a couple days ago, and so I played the song on REPEAT to dislodge it. For a while there, everything was a loop.

Lindsborg was, as the guidebook promised, "Sweden-themed." The legacy of a wave of emigration from that country in the nineteenth century and a craving for highway-tourism dollars in the twentieth. Blue-and-yellow flags hung in front of cabins that looked like they'd been ripped from a giant's cuckoo clock. Along the sidewalk, statues of painted horses kept watch on the empty street. Just past downtown, I drove by a restaurant with goats on the roof. These goats were shaggy like dogs, with skirts of matted hair that fell to their knees.

They ate the bright-green turf above the gutter, with one goat balanced precariously along the crease of the roof's spine.

A few miles later, I saw the castle, sticking out of the hill like a yellow snaggletooth. It took a while to get there, and on the way I felt like some errant vassal approaching his lord's domain.

I parked halfway up the hill. There was only one other car there, a white Lincoln with a black door Frankensteined on. The door didn't shut all the way, so its owner had it fastened with duct tape. Whoever had parked it there wasn't anywhere in sight.

I stuck the derringer in the pocket of my jacket. Bede was asleep. One of his paws hung limp under the crate's latch. When I got out, I shut the car door gently so I wouldn't wake him.

The castle was made up of a squat sandstone building beside a crenellated tower no more than two stories high. Blue skinks rolled in the dust at its base. About a half-mile away, a herd of cows was headed down to a creek, trotting in a perfect line toward a brown ribbon of water.

"Hey!"

I looked around but didn't see anyone.

"Up here!"

Two heads peeked over the fortifications.

"There's a ladder around the other side. Come on up!"

One of the heads waved a beer bottle to point me in the right direction. I found a big orange ladder leading all the way up to the top.

I climbed. The two heads reappeared above the tower and reached over to steady the ladder. I realized that I might have been too trusting, that this might be a prank and they were waiting to push me down and crack my back. But I made it to the top and found a hand to steady me as I straddled the gap-toothed crenellations.

An old man and a teenage boy greeted me as I brushed the yellow dust off my pants.

"I scared the shit out of you," the old man said. He had a big white mustache and held a rubber mallet, which he kept whacking against the meat of his thigh. He might have passed for a Norse god if it weren't for his snowbird tan, which made him look like he'd been pumped full of peanut butter. The teen had a bowl cut and wore a black T-shirt with a prism printed on it. A big pair of binoculars hung around his neck. Both the old man and the boy were drinking Corona Lights, and the old man set down the hammer to hand me one from the six-pack.

"Coronas for Coronado." His pronunciation of "Coronado" made it rhyme with "tornado."

"I'm Theron," the man said. "This is my grandson,

Kenny. If you're wanting some peace and quiet, just let me know, but I figured you might want some company. Kenny isn't very chatty, and I could always use someone to chew the fat with."

Kenny drank some of his beer and turned around to stare over the edge of the tower.

"You come out here often?" I asked.

"Every couple weeks or so when the weather is good. Prairie wizards like to stop by here. So we keep an eye out for them."

I thought he was talking about a kind of bird, something quailish or pheasantlike, but then he added, "Actually, I thought you might be one, until we saw your automobile. No offense. Your beard's not quite long enough yet, though."

"What's a prairie wizard?"

"You don't know them? Kenny, get out your phone and show him. Prairie wizards are these individuals who wander around, usually Vietnam vets. Living off the land. Living off the grid. Walking along the highway and shit. You haven't seen them? Big old bearded guys with backpacks? Sometimes they got a dirty-ass dog? Here, look."

He flipped through some pictures on his grandson's phone. The men were just as he described them. One had a long white beard and a camouflage bandanna, and he was trailed by a soggy pit bull. Another carried a crossbow and dragged a wild turkey by its neck. The photos were grainy, taken from far away and zoomed in.

"There's something about the castle that attracts them. There's the water pump, but it's got to be something more than that. An energy. I think they spread the word about it amongst themselves, and so they all have to see it if they come this way."

"I want to be one someday," Kenny said.

"No, you don't," Theron said.

"I think it would be cool."

"They come here pretty often. I'm surprised you haven't seen at least one. Keep an eye out the next time you stop for gas."

I told him I would, and handed the phone back to Kenny.

"Is this your first time to the castle?"

"Yeah. I just saw the Hole to Hell, and they all told me I should come out here."

"Oh, that shithole. Now, that's a tourist trap. I hope they didn't charge you anything."

"I liked it."

"It's just an old well. They're everywhere. I could show you twenty 'bottomless pits' between here and Kansas City."

I wanted to defend it, but I couldn't put together a case. He was right. There really wasn't anything all that special about the hole.

He must have seen my displeasure, because then he added, "Maybe it's gotten better. I didn't mean anything by it."

The boy held up the binoculars and scanned the fields. I searched them, too. The sun was low. Everything—the high grass, the gentle waves in the land, the fences and county roads—was cast in gold-orange light. It was easy to see how people could mistake the place for a city of gold and ruin themselves in pursuit of it.

"I see one," the boy said.

"Land, ho!" Theron yanked the binoculars off his neck.

"Nope. False alarm. Not a wizard. Just a jogger."

We watched the black blob bob away. I reached for my beer, and the bone of the gun poked my ribs.

"Hey, do you think you could tell me what kind of bullets I need for this?"

"This is a weird piece." He rubbed the skull with his thumb. "Ugly little guy. Probably custom. But it's a forty-five. I got a forty-five in my car. I could load it for you if you want."

Kenny kept watch, and Theron led me back down the tower to his busted Lincoln. He had four guns in his back seat, and several boxes of ammunition laid out in the trunk.

"Got to be ready for anything nowadays," he said

with a hint of embarrassment before showing me how to load the derringer.

"Now, these guys have a tendency to kick hard. Backfire sometimes, too. I know a girl who lost her oboe scholarship when her pocket pistol backfired so hard it broke her hand. She was trying to shoot one of those tube-men they use in car lots."

I told him I'd be careful, and he gave me two extra bullets, which I stuck in the front pocket of my black shirt.

"Go in peace to love and serve the Lord," he shouted across the parking lot as I climbed back into my car.

On my way out of town, I pulled up to a gas station and parked around the back, next to the tire air pump. I crushed up half a pill and mashed it into the last spoonful of Spam. I put the spoon in Bede's mouth. His teeth clacked against the plastic as he licked off the meat. When the Spam was gone, I filled the spoon with water and he drank it. I filled it again, and he drank that, too.

I had to wait a few minutes for the pill to kick in, so I went inside the gas station to find a new liner for the carrier. While I was at it, I bought a loaf of white bread.

I ate a piece in the checkout line. In my mouth, the bread screamed for butter. Bread without butter to me is a vegetable. I like to eat all my calories at once. I prefer to eat nothing or be faced with the opportunity to eat

everything. To be healthy, I take my big meal at different times of day. A morning feast one day, a night feast
the next to balance it out, and so on. I had eaten three
pieces by the time I got to the register.

I'd gone through a few T-shirts already, and I was
running out of clothes. I bought an XXL T-shirt that
read "This Grandpa Gets What He Wants," a declara-
tion rendered in pink, salami-like letters and enjambed
between "Gets" and "What." Back at the car, I cut the
shirt in half to get more use out of it, and I took a long,
dogleg strip out of one side (bearing "Gets") to wipe out
the crate. Now one half read "This Grand What." The
other: "pa He Wants."

Bede was dazed and lying on his back, showing the
strawlike hairs on his belly. The pill could have calmed
a creature eight times his size, so even half a dose was
enough to sedate him pretty quickly. Still, I had to be
careful. I put on the driving gloves and fished out the
drowsy coyote. Bede arched his back and pawed at
ghosts as I pulled him out and set him on the seat. I
removed the old liner (a paint-splattered undershirt) and
threw it into the trash. Fortunately, the coyote hadn't
been drinking much water and didn't produce much pee,
so I didn't have to change the lining that often. Which
was good, because this was very difficult, requiring that
I remove the animal from the carrier. I was able to do it
only when he was sedated, and had to calculate the tim-

ing just right, to make sure the pill had had enough time to kick in before I touched him. Fifteen minutes would do the trick. I did it about once a day, or whenever the smell got too bad.

I took the "pa He Wants" half and spread it out along the bottom of the crate. I set Bede back in the carrier and rinsed out my bucket with a water spigot on the side of the building. Filling the bucket with water, I was overcome with a peculiar sensation. Everything was familiar: the spigot, the black plastic buckets of violets, the yellow bags of salt. I had been there before.

I hadn't, though. But I had seen it, in one of the pictures of prairie wizards on the boy's phone. I was standing precisely where a wizard had stood.

I checked my map. Colorado wasn't far, and then, after that, Montana.

15

I first celebrated Mass in Bruno's church twelve years before I read about him in the newspaper. His parish was in the Diocese of O., but, owing to the rather arbitrary drawing of the diocese border, the church was relatively close to my own, in the Diocese of Lafayette. So I wasn't surprised when I received a call from him asking if I might cover a Sunday evening service at his parish. He called late at night, speaking with the theatrical hush of an actor in an old radio play, and though he gave no reason for the last-minute fill-in, I could only assume there'd been some family emergency. I didn't have to think too much about it. My parish offered no service at that time, and, even if he didn't explain himself, it was clear he was in need. From my years as his student and the past decade or so as diocese neighbors, I didn't have much affection for Bruno, but I figured I might need him to return the favor at some point. I told him sure, I could fill in for him, and that Sunday I drove out to his parish in O., a small church attached to a Catholic school.

At the time, I noticed nothing out of the ordinary. His parish was more old-school than mine, with an ornate baldachin and a border of Communion kneelers surrounding the altar. They had altar boys, which I wasn't accustomed to. The decision to have servers is left to each pastor. Some allow boys and girls to serve, others only boys. And others, including me, didn't care for or require the practice. (I keep—kept—my sanctuary pretty simple, with everything needed close at hand and a liturgical director to oversee the lectors and ushers and everything else.) Bruno's parish was boys-only. When I arrived, I found one of them in the sacristy. He introduced himself when he saw me, and then, rather strangely, took my hand and kissed the ring on my finger—a ring I had made myself, out of pewter. "I'm not the pope," I said, jerking my hand away, and he apologized and went off to arrange the water and oil.

Bruno was a pre–Vatican II guy. As I dressed myself in his sacristy, I looked over his trove of ecclesiastical gadgetry. A pearl-studded chalice that looked like something an elf had stolen from under a dragon's belly. An ornate monstrance that could have doubled as a back scratcher for a Borgia.

There, among Bruno's personal reliquary, I saw a strange wooden box. Inside, I found what must have been a hundred pins, the kind you'd wear on your lapel, all in the shape of electric guitars. These were done with great precision; you could tell that they were made for people who cared about the finer details of the instruments' anatomy and manufacture. Voluptuous blue jazz guitars, perky Stratocasters (I can play some, I'm from that generation). The prizes of the collection had been set into the velvet lining of the lid, pins with amethysts, garnets, and opals embedded in them, two or three made from real gold. I nearly stole one of the lesser pins, but I knew that someone with such a collection would be the kind of person who'd notice something missing, and I didn't want him to blame the altar boys. I shut the reliquary and resumed my duties.

We went about the Mass as usual. I was grateful to have the altar boy's help in the intricacies of a service at someone else's church, especially a church so different from my own. A dark and mostly empty church, with a Romanesque-esque severity I could appreciate, even if it wasn't my style. This church was full of dark pockets, and almost every surface was inscribed with a grim saint's face or fine spirals of filigree. I wondered if I should have added a few more touches of decoration to my worship space, to inspire a little more mystery.

The whole time, my assistant was as serious and solid as a policeman. Had he been ordained, the altar boy could have said the Mass on his own. When it was all over, he helped me put everything—the cruets, the paten, the crisp stacks of folded cloth—back in place. After he took off his cassock, I saw something gleam on the collar of his shirt: a red Gibson Flying V. I thanked him for his help, and the boy left the sacristy and stepped out into the dark.

I filled in for Bruno two or three more times after that, once with the same altar boy, but I never saw the box of pins after that, nor did the boy try to kiss my ring again. More and more, the duties of pastoral work and my precarious relationship with the bishop occupied most of my attention, and I shoved these strange signs down into my memory's darker catacombs. But years later, when I read about what he'd done to those two boys in his congregation, the pins and the ring came back to me immediately, revived like crazed zombie Lazaruses. Should I have said something to someone? Should I have seen something in it? I should have.

These are the things I thought about when I lay in bed for a week. Pretending to be sick, but also actually sick, just not in the way I told my secretary. I thought about this and I thought about quitting. I found my pewter ring and flushed it down the toilet.

16

I counted five dead deer, three dead raccoons, a dead coyote, and two white wooden crosses between Lindsborg and Hays. It was getting to be time to let the coyote go, but I didn't want to let him off anywhere near roadkill, any spot where he was more likely to be hit again. I was holding out for Colorado.

A road is a stripe of death. It requires a streamlined apocalypse to be born: hacking down forests, leveling the ground, blasting through layers of rock. Then, once the road is there, it keeps on killing until it becomes a trail marked by white crosses and piles of deer, stiff raccoons, overturned possum, armadillo bowls, and coyote pelts. Patches of mashed, illegible gore. All killed by machines that run on the black rot of billions of microscopic creatures, the dead that power death.

A road is a long absence, a black line crossing things out.

I needed to practice, at least once, now that I had the bullets. A couple miles outside of Hays, I took a lonely exit and followed it onto a frontage road. I found an empty stretch where I could park, and, after practicing loading the gun, I stacked a few empty tuna cans on a fence post. I turned off the safety, checked the nubs of the sights, and fired.

It was incredibly loud. The gun shook the bones in my hand, leaving it painfully sore for the rest of the day, like I'd slammed it in the car door.

As for my marksmanship, the tower of tuna cans stood unmoved. But I wasn't worried—I'd get too close to miss.

I saw a hitchhiker just across the state border. For a moment I thought he might be a prairie wizard. But he was a young man, with a long blond ponytail and a giant backpack covered in patches that gave him the rectangular outline of a refrigerator.

Hitchhikers are anachronisms. So are priests. I think it's safe to say hitchhikers have more in common with Jesus than most priests do. I picked him up.

By now, most of my clothes were dirty. I'd been wearing a big gray T-shirt smeared with paint stains, the shirt I'd wear when working on an art project. I'd thrown my black shirt and collar into the back, on top of the carrier, after I left the castle. To make room for my passenger, I tossed a few other odds and ends from the front seat back there and hid the gun under the books.

The hitchhiker nestled his backpack in the footwell and climbed in.

He smelled like old bananas. I offered him a bottle of water, but he had his own canteen.

"Ooh, Prince," he said as I pulled us back onto the road. He picked up the yellow CD case under the green envelope.

He said he was going to Boulder.

"My brother lives there," he says. "One of my brothers. I'm one of ten. Grew up Mormon."

I told him I was from a big family, too.

"Where are they?"

"They're all dead."

"Oh. I'm sorry."

"I'm old. And I was the youngest."

Just a few miles from where I picked him up, the traffic slowed to a stop. There'd been an accident—I could see the lights of police cars up ahead.

The hitchhiker looked around the back seat.

"Dog or cat?"

"Dog."

He bent over to peek in.

"He's a funny-looking little dude. Rescue?"

"Yeah."

He wanted a dog, he said. He wanted to live in a tiny house. The kind you could mount on a flatbed trailer. Just him and a dog and possibly a boyfriend, if he could find someone who wanted to live in a tiny house with a dog.

"You can make them really small. Put storage under

the stairs, loft the bed—there are all kinds of solutions to save space. Then you're not bogged down with a mortgage or any of that shit. You can just go where you please. I've been saving up. My brother will help me build it, on his land."

"Is your brother still Mormon?"

"We both left the church around the same time. Which amounts to leaving your family. It was hard for us. Both young and gay and Mormon. We call ourselves the Latter-gay Saints. We have each other, which is better than most of us get. But I still miss my parents. I miss my sisters. It sucks. Like, I had to leave behind the rest of my life. Family is, like, the whole thing for us Mormons, and my family is pretty conservative. You get that programmed into you from day one, and now I'm, like, Will I ever be happy? When that's your whole upbringing, can you really ever get away from it? Will it ever get out of my system?"

I touched his hand to comfort him.

"I have a friend who was a priest, but then he fell in love with a man and quit. I think he's really happy now. I think you can make a new family."

"Yeah, I know."

I'd fallen into a priestly mode. I tried to communicate my care as best I could, to give him a real quality of attention. I gave him some meaningful eye contact just as a motorcycle rushed past us on the shoulder.

He leaned over and kissed me on the mouth. His hair smelled like wood smoke, and there was still the banana smell.

I pulled away.

"Oh, I'm sorry," he said. "I just got the vibe. I thought you were talking about yourself?" He pointed to the shirt balled up on the carrier.

I told him it was okay.

The traffic picked back up. He fell asleep, and we rode for another two hours or so before he woke up and told me to let him off at Aurora. I pulled over and gave him twenty dollars. He looked at the twenty and then reached into the pouch of his hooded sweatshirt and handed me a square of tinfoil.

"It's a brownie. It'll get you a pretty intense body-high. Don't eat it all at once."

He got out of the car and slung his enormous pack onto his back. I watched the anchorite waddle off into the woods, and then started the car back up.

17

I think the holiest people are the ones who can leave everything behind in search of a true life. The Apostles. St. Antony, Evagrius, and the other Desert Fathers and Mothers. Anna. The prairie wizards. The hitchhiker. I'm fascinated by them, I think, because I've always wanted to be like them and have always fallen short.

In 2004 (or was it 2005?), a nurse in my congregation traveled to Haiti on a Rotary Club medical trip, along with a number of doctors, other nurses, and one or two brave dentists. When the nurse returned, she arranged for a meeting with me, during which she told me she found herself changed by the experience and could think of nothing else. The island plagued her dreams, which had become increasingly populated by people speaking in French, or what sounded like French—she barely knew the language, and had no facility with the Haitian Creole dialect. She set to the task of arranging for our parish to adopt a sister parish somewhere on the island. She gave a speech at the end of a Sunday Mass describing in great detail the horrors and beauties she had witnessed there. She spoke of children with worms coming out of their noses and women dying of treatable diseases. After a little resistance from the parish board, it was decided that St. Antony's would fund a trip to the town, sending our congregation's doctors, along with a few of the nurse's companions who'd gone on the original Rotary Club trip. Of course the nurse went with them, and this time she returned with more photographs and accounts of the people they had helped. "Helped" being, by her account, barely anything and, at best, only temporary, given the bottomless need in the area, a poor town in the world's poorest nation.

It was around this time that people in my congregation began to register certain changes in her appearance and demeanor. She refrained entirely from dining in restaurants, refusing all invitations to do so. She grew difficult to talk to, having almost no patience for pleasantries and showing no sympathy for the complaints of others. And she began dressing very simply, wearing old jeans, baggy sweatshirts, disintegrating tennis shoes. I remember seeing her in the same shirt almost all the time, a faded sweatshirt commemorating a 5k run from 1992. This—her clothing—was the only thing I noticed at the time. The other details wouldn't come to me until later, once her life began to change more dramatically and I could not escape the gossip that followed her. But what I saw then was a person awakening to something, some higher, greater purpose. I'll admit, I was pulled into her mission, too, sucked into the wake of her resolve—and with great enthusiasm, bordering on obsession. I mirrored her. (If my soul were to take the form of an everyday object, that is what it would be. Paul was a curtain. The nurse was a hammer. I'm a mirror, dimly.)

This was just a couple years after I learned about Bruno, and I needed something to pour my energy into, to renew my faith that the Church could do some good in the world. For weeks, the nurse and I met every other day, talking about the next steps in our program, how best to meet the needs of our sister parish, and soon it was decided not only that we would send another team of doctors to Plaisance (that was the name of the town), but that I would join them, too, the thought being that I would be able to cement the bond between our parishes, as well as witness and assess their needs firsthand.

And so, after another round of meetings and fundraising, I set out for Haiti.

After we'd landed in Port-au-Prince, we piled into an old conversion van and one of the nurse's local contacts drove us out to the country. Much of the ride took us by the green sea and a number of fruit farms. Five or six hours later, we arrived in town and were dropped off at the little white church, our sister parish.

We brought with us a huge quantity of over-the-counter medicine, and when I got there, I found a bulk bottle of aspirin had come open during the flight, filling my clothes with small white pills. It looked like a huge moth had laid its eggs in my suitcase.

The doctors set to work at their weeklong clinic. I spent most of my time in triage, alongside the nurse. Together we appraised the sick, moved them up and down in a line that always grew, was a creature unto itself, a millipede with hundreds of arms, legs, hearts, every illness and every ailment. A single creature made of suffering itself, it seemed to me.

But this is not a complete portrait. I mostly saw people, normal people, living their lives. Teenagers smoking. Children playing soccer. Circles of men passing around bottles of Scotch whisky and joking with one another. I'd expected something hellish (and saw plenty of terrible things), but I was most disarmed by the banality. I realized I had, up to that point, willfully ignored this. I'd chosen unimaginable horror so I wouldn't have to reckon with imaginable pain.

I became close with the pastor and a local doctor, a man and woman of sterling credentials (he'd received a master's in divinity at Yale; she had worked for UNICEF before "retiring" to her home village and an exhausting private practice sustained by the savings from her previous employment). Together the three of us, joined from time to time by the nurse, stayed up late, talking about John Henry Newman's autobiography, Thomas

Merton, and Elvis. Before I departed, the pastor gave me his copy of a collection of the poems of Judah Halevi, a medieval Jewish poet whose works he'd studied. I told him I couldn't take it, but he insisted, swearing he'd copied them down in his notebooks anyway. I barely looked at it when he gave it to me. Later, when I got back, I opened it and found that the poems were written entirely in Hebrew. I'd been to Israel just one time, and I don't know any Hebrew. I stood there and stared stupidly at the beautiful, mysterious lines. I still have the book. It's in the back seat somewhere.

One night, while we drank beer in the sacristy, a bunch of aspirin fell out of my sleeves. The pastor picked one up and said, "You're snowing." He pinched the pill and flicked it into the nave.

By the end of the week, I could think of nothing but returning to the town. For the duration of the plane ride home, the nurse and I assessed our impressions and devised the next step in our plans.

About a month after our return, we approached the board with a proposal to build a well. This was met with some resistance by the more conservative members of the parish council, but we managed to put a plan in place to finance the digging and contract a company from a nearby town.

The nurse had me over to her apartment to celebrate the night the board approved the plans. I'd been there a few times before. It'd been a comfortable, unremarkable home, decorated with photos from their travels and Ansel Adams prints of veiny leaves and sentimental trees. But the place was now unrecognizable to me. Her walls had been stripped down and painted white—there was almost nothing on them except some photographs of Haiti and photocopies of the well plans taped above a writing desk. We drank whiskey and sat on the floor, near the desk. Her husband, an architect who helped draft the plans, drank with us. "We're into minimalism now," he said, waving his hands up towards the walls.

"How do you feel about all this?" I asked him when the nurse got up to use the bathroom.

"I think it's just the first flush. I'm guessing it's like any romance, and it'll cool off a little." He pressed a hand against the bare wall. "She won't even let me have a TV!"

We spent the rest of the night talking about Plaisance. What our next move would be. How we'd raise more money. How we might build a new school, which was the nurse's grand vision.

While we talked, a blue housefly buzzed around us, landing on our knees, in our hair, on the rims of our glasses.

The nurse reached for a spoon on the desk and held it in her lap for a while. When the fly landed on the floor near her foot, she raised the spoon and quickly slammed it down. She lifted the spoon, and the fly's body lay there upturned, its legs folded against its burst heart.

A year later, I was back in Plaisance with the nurse and our cohort. One night, before we returned to the sanctuary space where we slept, she and I went on a walk to take another look at the well. The sun was skating down past the hills, and some kids were playing soccer in the field in front of us.

She removed a pack of cigarettes from her pocket and proceeded to smoke. I must have seen her smoke before that, but this was the first time I can recall. The nurse stood there, smoking, and we watched the kids kick the ball around.

I asked if I could bum a cigarette, and she gave me one. I was never a smoker, but in that moment she made it look impossibly cool. I wanted what she had.

"This is my life now," she said, dead serious. She was wearing the same 5k sweatshirt. The "5" and the "k" had hairy arms and legs and their own running shoes. Side by side, they tore through the tape of the finish line with their thin arms raised in exhausted triumph.

The kids' soccer ball rolled over to our feet. She shouted something in French and kicked it back. The children laughed and repeated whatever it was she said, she smiled and put out her cigarette, and we walked down to the well together.

You get to the end and you have to look at your life and ask yourself: Did I do anything good? Did I truly help anybody? An examination of conscience before you step into that last dark booth.

If I've done anything good, the well is the best of it. That hole in the ground, twin to the bottomless pit in Kansas, might be the only good thing, the only thing of real goodness, that I have put my name on. I wish we had dug two.

We flew back to Indiana the next morning. After this trip, something changed in our parish, and our commitment to our mission in Haiti began to falter. The conservative council members (no doubt the same ones who tattled on me to the bishop when we held the wake) won out. They began raising irritating questions: Why did we have to go so far to find the poor? Couldn't we help those in need in our community? In our parish?

I resisted them for a while, but soon it was clear that many felt this way. They weren't entirely off-base, either. I was their pastor, entrusted to serve them. I had a responsibility to them, I thought, and I found myself persuaded by their arguments. Now I think that I should have pushed back more, that maybe my responsibility was to call on them to help others. But at the time I didn't see it this way, and for that I have some real shame.

So began the gradual slide in our efforts, which, after

another medical trip, trickled into a mere yearly fish fry and the occasional check. Haiti (like Paul, and like the trouble with Bruno) drifted away from me, became more like a raft than an island, so to speak, floating farther out into the water until it was gone.

I saw less and less of the nurse, too. Undeterred by our weakness, she went to Haiti with doctors from other churches, using her growing expertise and contacts to make herself an indispensable fixer. For a while I didn't see her at Mass, and soon I heard she'd divorced her husband. Not long after that, I was told she moved to Haiti permanently.

She's still there, for all I know.

18

I haven't been completely honest with you. Which is to say, me.

This afternoon I drove into the suburbs of Denver, looking for the address on the envelope. I'd stopped earlier, outside a diner, where a man pulling weeds pointed the way with some crabgrass. His idiosyncratic landmarks ("the ugly house," a "windmill thing") made me think of stopping again and asking someone else, but before long I wound up on the right street (sure enough, the ugly house was, in fact, ugly, painted algae green).

The houses were mostly the same, variations on a wooden ranch with skinny saplings dotting the yard. It was hard for me to imagine my friend living here.

I found the address and parked the car on the street. In the yard was a concrete bear with flowers growing out of a hole in its back.

Before I got out, I grabbed the green envelope from the cup holder and pulled out the letter inside.

Dear Dan,

Forgive the epistle—I know it's dramatic, but I needed a way to put my thoughts together at my own pace. As I write this, the sun is coming up and the whole world is the color of a nectarine. Tim's asleep upstairs, and I'm sitting outside, listening to birds in my robe and slippers, putting off getting to the point.

I don't know how much you knew, or know, about what happened to me when we were at John Bosco's. When I first arrived, a year before you, I was a lonely kid. I didn't have the same kind of protection or support you or the other boys had. James Bruno knew about my parents and sought me out right away. He told me he'd keep an eye out for me—his parents were dead, too, he said, and he had a group of a few other boys he looked after who'd gone through something similar. He showed me how to play his guitar and gave me pot and new LPs. He got me drunk for the first time in his room and made me sit on his lap. That night he raped me. After that first time, he told me I was his boyfriend, and I liked that. This happened over and over for most of my first year there. He'd pull me out of class, made me stay with him over the holidays. Sometimes I wanted it, even, and sought him out, flirted. After a year, I was having what I now know were panic attacks, and I stopped seeing him. Mr. Patton—the handyman, you remember him?—had some sense of what had happened, and he gave me a place to go when I was too afraid of James. For a long time, I told myself it had been a real relationship, and I ruled out the possibility that he might still be doing this to other people, which was cowardly of me, a real sin, knowing what he did later to the boys in his congregation. (James harassed me on and off for years. I thought he was trying to threaten our mutually assured destruction if it came out he was gay; I didn't know he was something else entirely.) Even when I became a priest, I couldn't think about it head-on, though I think it was why I came back to Indiana. I felt better knowing where he was, strangely, and at the same time it was good to have you between him and me, geographically.

It messed me up for a long time, and I could never find a way to tell you. Talking about it seemed to make it real, and worse. You and I, with our via negativa fetish, always hated to put words on things, and I've always felt that you were a person I could sit in silence with and that would be enough.

Even without telling you these things, I always felt that you loved and accepted me no matter what I did or what happened to me, and that's why I feel like I can tell you all this now, half a century later. You always reminded me of God that way, a kind of weird, artsy guy whose love I needed but could never understand.

Anyway, I want you to know this, and I want to talk more about it with you, on the phone or, even better, here. I don't know why you don't just move here (our offer still stands, by the way), but you were always a flagellant. You'd wear a hair shirt if you could. Stop that. Come and see me and Tim.

Love,
Paul

I folded the letter up and carefully placed it back in the envelope. I got out of the car and almost rang the doorbell, but before I did I doubled back and changed into my shirt and collar. I pulled my jean jacket over it to cover up the wrinkles.

A short, skinny man answered the door. I hadn't seen him since his wedding.

"Tim?" I said. "I'm Dan. Paul's friend?"

He looked me over and gave me a puzzled smile.

"I know who you are, Dan. What are you doing here?"

"I'm on my way to Seattle. I thought I'd come by. Say hi."

"Um. Sure. Come in. Let me get your jacket."

He opened the coat closet, and I glimpsed something shiny in the nest of scarves and hats above the hangers.

"No, it's okay. It's a little chilly."

"This beard is working for you. You look like Walt Whitman. Or Rutherford B. Hayes."

"Thanks."

"You hungry? Can I get you a drink? It's cocktail hour over here."

Tim picked up a glass with whiskey and ice chattering in it, from a table in the foyer.

"Sure."

He poured me a drink and led me through the house. Pictures of him and Paul covered the walls. My friend stared back at me from the Grand Canyon, a few mountaintops, a number of white, sandy beaches and airbrushed sunsets. If I hadn't known him, I would have thought the smiles to be fake and cheesy, but that was how Paul had actually smiled, and I could tell he was happy.

Tim led me to a pair of chairs in the backyard. You could see the big maroon mountains from them. They had a suction to them that made it hard to look at anything else.

"You've lost weight." I said. "You're so little now."

"Yeah. I still feel like it's on me." He grabbed at an invisible belly. "Never feels like I really lost anything. Mirrors still startle me."

He took a drink.

"Gotta say, I'm surprised to see you, Dan."

"I should have let you know I was coming, I know. I just didn't know how soon I'd get here."

"No. I mean, I thought I'd see you at the funeral. Or before then."

"Yeah."

"I know Paul wrote to you," Tim said. "I assume he mentioned how sick he was."

"He didn't say anything about that."

"That's like him, I guess. He was always circling around things."

Did Tim know as much as I did? Did he know about Bruno? I'd figured he would, but now I wasn't so sure. If Paul could withhold it from me for fifty years, he could keep it from Tim for ten.

"Paul really loved you," Tim said. "The way he put things, it sounded like you loved him, too."

The mountains appeared to be cut out of one vast maroon sheet of construction paper, and as the sun began to set, the shadows made their slow, purple progress down the slopes.

"It's all right. It's all right." He disappeared into the house and came back with some Kleenex, which he handed to me.

"It's good you came. I'll write down the directions to the grave so you can see it on your way out of town."

He waited a minute for me to calm down, and the conversation turned to other matters.

"You've been retired for about six years, right? They have you set up somewhere nice?"

"Yeah. A little church in Alexandria. Indiana. Not the one with the lighthouse. Or the library. I wish it was. About fifteen miles from Paul's old parish."

"I know where that is. I was in Noblesville when I met Paul. They taking care of you okay?"

"Oh yeah." I adjusted myself in the chair so it wouldn't hurt my back so much. "Are you retired?"

"Semi. There's a Unitarian church not far from here. I lead a service every now and then, fill in for the pastor. And I help a little with organizing the General Assembly."

"Those mountains are something."

"Yeah." He pinched and pulled at the extra skin hanging off his elbow. He had a lot of it. "I just think I should say this. I really don't want to dig anything up for you. But you're here, and I think you should know. He was serious about the offer. He and I'd talked it over for a while, after he heard you were retiring. I was just fine with it. We'd cleared out the room. He really wanted you here. Not hearing from you really hurt him."

The solidity of the mountains. From far away, everything flattens into just one color. Your brain can't pick up on all the details. You just read the values. The best painters reproduced this. Vermeer and Rembrandt and Whistler and Caspar David Friedrich.

"You look a little zonked. Sure you don't want to crash here? You can stay as long as you need to."

"That's really kind. But I think I should hit the road pretty soon."

I reached into my pocket and took out the brownie.

"Hey, I have this pot brownie. Do you want to eat it with me?"

"Hell, why not? It's been too long since I got high."

I unwrapped it and pulled off a corner.

"I think you only eat a little bit."

"I know how it works," he said. "The high priest— that's what Paul always called himself whenever we smoked pot." He smiled the way he and Paul did in the photographs.

I gave him the corner and pulled off a hunk of my own, and the two of us ate of it. We sat there for another hour. My stomach began to feel like a lava lamp. We talked about things he and Paul had done, what Paul had been up to before his diagnosis, and Tim went back in a couple times, to get a stereo speaker, more Kleenex, and more whiskey. He mixed a couple of Manhattans and stirred them with a spoon. He kept the spoon in his glass, and the more he drank, the more it began to ring the glass like a bell.

I needed to know how much Tim knew.

"Did Paul ever say anything about a priest named James Bruno?"

"Oh yeah. Around when we met, he said he'd told me that for a long time he'd been harassed by one of the conservatives near your parish who'd taught back at John Bosco's, and then, years later, he found out he'd been a pedophile. Paul thought this guy was trying to leverage his sexuality against him, hold it over Paul's head in case he ever caught on to anything, but Paul couldn't see that at the time—he said he thought he was just a closeted bully who'd become kind of obsessed with him. My guess was that this Bruno guy thought Paul might've seen something back in the seminary that Paul could use against him, but Paul said he couldn't remember anything like that, and that was where we left it. But you know how he was about his childhood, the foster families and everything. He liked to keep that stuff in the vault. I couldn't ever ask about it directly, I could only pick up the crumbs. I'm still jealous of all your shared history. Anyway, all he said was that once he heard the news he started seriously thinking about quitting. He'd say it was me that really made him quit, but the news about this Bruno guy really seemed to give him that first push."

"Bruno pulled the same moves on me, always bringing up how close I was with Paul. I didn't pick up on it then, either. I think I should have noticed something."

"It's all a little easier in retrospect. I'm sure that guy did whatever he could to cover his tracks. It's how they work."

"Did he ever say anything else about John Bosco's?"

"No, just that that was where he met you. You ever see anything suspicious when you were there?"

"Not really."

So he didn't know everything that had happened to Paul. It's ugly, but I felt a peculiar glee. Paul had told me and not Tim. But this perverse delight quickly turned to visceral guilt. I was the only person in the world who knew, and I'd done nothing.

The mountains turned orange dusted with pink— colossal nectarines, just like Paul said. Tim offered again to let me stay the night in the guest room, but I said I had to get back on the road. I told him to keep the rest of the brownie, and he gave me the directions to the cemetery.

"You're all comfortable," I told him. "I'll just let myself out."

He nodded and, after hugging me goodbye, leaned back into his chair and looked out at the mountains.

"Please take care of yourself, Dan."

Before I left the house, I peeked back into the coat closet. Along the shelf above the hangers I saw the same little chrome flash I'd noticed earlier. It was Frank, the ukulele, tucked into a box with a photo album and a nest of rosaries. The sticker was still there, but the namesake saint had faded into a bald and faintly bearded ghost.

I couldn't steal it, though I wanted to, badly.

Instead, I took out my pocketknife and unfolded the tiny scissors. I detuned one of the strings until it was slack and cut it free.

Catholics get a lot of shit for our obsession with relics. Admittedly, we have a tendency to go overboard. I've already mentioned our bottles of Lourdes water and other popular papist souvenirs, and then there are the true relics: the proliferating pieces of the True Cross, the piles of sacred bones, and the innumerable shreds of shrouds and veils bearing only a vague resemblance to the Savior or his beloved mom. By the sixteenth century, there were so many churches claiming to hold vials of Mary's breast-milk that Calvin famously joked that, even if the Virgin were a cow, it would have been tough for her to produce that much. Still, maybe I've been too hard on this tradition. Within reason, I think there is something special about it. These scraps of bone and cloth remind us that the saints once had bodies that needed covering, that they were real and not just stories, even if that's what they have become in the end.

Because, of course, the saints were just people like us. All the good dead are saints, and they leave us relics, too.

Once I'd made it out the door and back to the car, I looped the string around my wrist and tied it with a firm square knot, which I doubled, then tripled, until I was sure it would hold.

19

It was late when I got to the cemetery. I dug out my flashlight and poked around in the dark, shining my light on the headstones and tarnished statues of angels. I looked for the kind of grave I thought Paul would want— something simple, without fanfare. This, of course, made my task all the more difficult. I was an idiot not to have asked Tim where in the cemetery I could find him, but I took his lack of specification to mean that the grave was not extraordinary, or located somewhere unusual. Though it also could also have meant he was, like me, a little high.

The cemetery was a maze, which suited Paul. He had a theory that the world could be divided into two categories. There were labyrinths, and there were deserts, and that was about it. The moon, he said, was a desert. The Internet was a labyrinth. America was a desert, generally. Books were, for the most part, labyrinths, except for two, maybe three books of poetry that were deserts.

"What about the sea?" I asked.

"A desert, easily."

"A desert of water?"

"If you could drink sand, would a desert still be a desert?"

"What about people?"

"Labyrinths. Mazes of veins, nerves, intestines. The brain is a labyrinth. The heart is a labyrinth."

The two of us made a real labyrinth once, to prepare our parishes (and, perhaps, more selfishly, ourselves) for Lent. We made two, actually, one for each of our churches. I copied the design from a library book and made a transparency, which we traced onto two big burlap sheets that took up most of the narthex. Once they'd dried, we gave them a test run, each of us walking through his own painted maze, circling closer and closer to our destinations.

By this point, his theory (too dualistic for my tastes) had long been established. When we were done walking the mazes, I asked him what our labyrinths were, deserts or labyrinths.

"Deserts," he said, straight-faced, and we rolled up his desert-maze and stuck it in his truck.

By now it was completely dark out, and it would, I realized, take me hours to find him without directions. I decided I'd sleep at the cemetery and look for the grave in the morning. I parked across the street, so I wouldn't arouse the suspicion of any patrolling cops, and brought my things through the gates.

This took two trips. I went back to retrieve the carrier and crack the windows to air out the terrible odor that had been building up.

The letter was where I'd left it. Counting that afternoon, I'd only ever read it twice. It came to me just two years ago—a year before Paul died. Reading it that first time, I'd felt I already knew what he had to say. I thought about writing back right away, or calling, but I told myself that the best thing to do was just get in the car and drive to him, the way we used to when we were younger. But my shame paralyzed me. I never went, and then he died.

To lend myself some cover, I set up my tent on a patch of grass between two trees. Not wanting to piss on the dead, I also brought my bucket, which I hung from a low branch. Once everything was in place, I moved Bede's crate close to the tent.

On a whim, I decided to open it. I stood from the side, so the creature wouldn't be facing me directly once it was free, then popped the latch and swung open the wire door. I stood back and watched.

Nothing happened for a while. Then the coyote's nose stuck out, a scaly plum. Then a paw, and soon Bede was limping out.

This was not, admittedly, an ideal place to liberate him. But I don't think that was my intention. Whatever I was thinking, there was no need to worry about it, because he went no farther than a few steps before he curled up in the grass.

I washed the carrier out with water from my jug and fed him a can of tuna. While he ate, I opened another can for myself. We sat there, eating, and I looked out at the graves and the grass and trees above the dead that were also the dead. That might, in a couple years, be Paul.

Not long after that, I climbed into the tent and tried to get some sleep. A few minutes later, I heard something against the side of the tent. Bristly hairs poked through the mesh. Bede was resting against the side, taking cover from the wind.

In the middle of the night, I got up to piss in the bucket. The lights of the nearby city bleached out the stars and kept the sky dark purple. When I was finished, I turned to find the coyote staring back at me. His eyes looked like radioactive moons, and for a moment I was truly afraid of him.

I looked down and saw he had something in his mouth. A ram's horn. A shofar.

He pulled it close to him, and curled up again.

And then he went back to sleep, and I did, too.

※

My sister Agnes died three years ago in a retirement center in Fort Wayne. She was eighty-three, and her husband had died two years before her. Her children, my niece and nephew, only ten years younger than me, asked me to perform the service. Which I did, in a small church near the retirement home where she died (St. Isabel? St. Isidore?), a church with very thin, very long stained-glass windows with scenes from the Gospels going all the way up. Jesus reviving Lazarus. God reaching through a hole in the heavens like some celestial catfish-noodler. I thought I could make out a camel in one of the windows, but I couldn't raise my head enough to be sure without looking completely unhinged. Who could see the images way up there? Why would they put them so high? This is what I thought about all through the service.

My brother Richard died two years before that, also near Fort Wayne, and his death came on the heels of my brother Michael's death, only three months prior. September and June. Both services were held in their home parish, where they'd both attended. I celebrated (a terrible word for it) both funerals, which, in my memory, is one funeral. I remember things—a line from the liturgy ("As the hind thirsts for running waters, so my soul longs for you, O God"), a child in the second row chewing a large quantity of gum so hard that I could see all the muscles in his head—but when, in which service any of this happened, I can't for the life of me remember.

These last three made up the second wave of death to course through my family. The first started five years earlier and took my sisters Elaine, Kate, and Brigid, one right after the other. Elaine had breast cancer; Kate and Brigid died of complications related to their old age. Unlike with my brothers, I recall these services with great clarity. Brigid's funeral in Tulsa (a reading from Romans), Elaine's and Kate's in St. Louis, where they lived next door to one another. Even though both of these were in the same church, like Ricky and Mike, for some reason I'm nevertheless able to disentangle the scenes. Mike reading from Job (Elaine's). A giant white moth in the sacristy (Kate's).

My mother's funeral was in the parish I grew up in. I hadn't been back to that church since I was a teenager. I had remembered it as being vast, its darkness impenetrable. Now it was quaint. I felt much too large, like an adult in a kindergarten classroom surrounded by tiny chairs and desks. Paul said the Mass, and as I knelt in the pew and looked up from the height I'd been as a child, everything fell into place. I celebrated my brother's funeral. I read the responsorial psalm at my mother's ("No one who waits for you, O Lord, will ever be put to shame"). My brother Patrick died from complications of AIDS in the early nineties. He lived in Miami, and I will always think of Florida as a land of death and blindness. Patrick was everyone's favorite, and mine. His funeral was in Florida, in a pink-and-orange church. My father's death came just two months after I was ordained, in 1973. At my mother's insistence, I sat among the other priests in my vestments, as a co-celebrant. I worried myself with the notion that, since he'd been the coroner, his death would be incorrectly processed somehow. There was a deputy, of course, but I stayed up the night before, convinced that there would be something wrong with the death certificate, or that his body wouldn't be in the casket when we received it. Even during the service, which was open-casket, I suspected that the body lying there, with its sagging cheeks, tangerine skin, and flat mouth, wasn't his, that there had been some mix-up and that we would have to do the whole thing all over again.

My brother Fred died in the Korean War—I was three years old and did not celebrate that one. The church was big and dark, and I held on to my sister until it was over.

I woke to someone shaking the poles of my tent.

"Excuse me, sir," a voice said. "But you can't sleep here."

I got out. The sun was coming up, pinkening the

tombstones and mausoleums. A security guard stood there, leaning on a massive headstone for a "beloved mother" named Mabel Stapp who'd died in the 1970s. The guard looked pretty strong, like she could have been a lumberjack or a gym teacher.

Bede had run off in the night. The slats on the fence were too tight for him to slip through, which meant he was still somewhere in the cemetery. But I'd have to look for him later.

She tapped the empty carrier with her shoe. "You have a dog around here somewhere?"

"I use that to carry my stuff."

"You're a minister?"

"Yeah. A Catholic priest."

I explained my situation.

"I can help you look," she said, and the two of us set out to find the tombstone.

"I've got nothing else going on," she said, suddenly grinning at me. "Things are pretty dead here."

For the pilgrims of the Middle Ages, it wasn't unusual to spend a night on a saint's tomb in the hope that its occupant might help cure their ailments or forgive their sins. When I camped out at the graveyard, I didn't think I was doing this—it only occurred to me later, as I drove away. In any case, it didn't work. My neck, back, and leg still ached. I didn't feel forgiven, either.

"Ever see any ghosts?" I asked as we walked between the graves.

"Did you say 'goats'? Or 'ghosts'?"

"Ghosts."

"No. We did use to have goats, though. That's what I thought you said."

She explained that, as recently as a year ago, they had had five or six goats on the grounds, mostly there as sentient lawn mowers.

"They were pretty popular. Some people would just come and hang out and watch them for a few hours. It made the cemetery more like a park. My boyfriend and I used to do it sometimes. They were cute. You could feed them birdseed. They'd eat carrots right out of your hand."

The graves, reflecting the early sunlight, looked like white crumbs. We came to a borough where the tombstones had winged skulls scratched into them. "Purple Rain" was still stuck in my head. It was becoming a problem. If anything, playing it on repeat had only made it worse. No sign of Paul. Or Bede.

"And then, one day, they found them all dead. Someone had brought in their dog and sicced it on them. It just ran around and killed them and didn't even eat them. Someone called the cops, but the guy and the dog left before they got there. That's actually why they hired me. But they haven't brought the goats back. The goats had these holes in their necks, like they'd been vampired. Their eyes were open. The groundskeeper showed me the pictures of them. He was the one who raised them."

We came to a statue of a glum angel with a plastic bag trembling by her sandals. The guard bent over to grab the bag, but instead of crumpling it up and stuffing it in her pocket, she pulled it over the angel's head.

"I'm sorry, but this one is too spooky."

She returned to the subject of the groundskeeper and his goats. "He's still sad about it. He calls them his kids, which is what you call baby goats, but I think he really means they were his *kids*. He gave them their own little funeral and everything. He said about forty or fifty people showed up. They're buried behind the guardhouse."

We circled around the graveyard until we found ourselves back near the trees where I'd camped. Paul's grave, it turned out, wasn't far from where I'd slept. Twenty yards away at the most.

"Here he is," I said.

His stone was simple, like I guessed it would be: a small brick embedded into the ground, his name and hyphenated dates.

"I'm sorry. I'll leave you alone."

She put a hand on my shoulder, and then I broke down. A pair of squirrels shook the branches above our heads. And under it all, behind everything, that song.

"There, there," the guard said. "There, there, there."

I checked the carrier when I got back. Bede was inside, sleeping. I woke him as I closed the door and managed to set the latch just before I saw his teeth.

The goat's horn was lying there in the grass. I picked it up and put it in my pocket before I tore everything down.

With the car packed, I took a pencil from the glove compartment and tore out a blank page from the back of Origen, careful to find a part Bede hadn't puked on. I took these things back to Paul's gravestone, pressed the paper against the engraving, and made a rubbing. I couldn't fit all of his name on the page, just the bottom halves of the letters and the pair of dates. This decapitated half of his name looked like an archaeological fragment, the last scrap of a forgotten language.

I brought the page back to the car, folded it in half, and stuck the letter inside it.

20

Before I drove off, I asked the guard if she could direct me to the Animal Control Center.

"Oh yeah. We call them over all the time."

She wrote down the directions and added, "Say hi to Tamar for me."

I told her I would, and left.

Animal Control, it turned out, was just two or three miles away. I parked the car and brought the carrier into the ugly concrete building with me.

Only one person was on duty. A middle-aged woman with blue hair wandered among racks of cages, mostly empty, a few occupied by the occasional cat or, as was the case with one, a raccoon. Lodged in the corner, in a carrier much like Bede's, was a large gray owl with orange eyes and a head the size and shape of a paper valentine.

"What can I do for you?" the woman asked, speaking with a throaty accent I thought might be French.

I told her my predicament, expressing my hope that they might be able to relocate the coyote. As I spoke, I saw that her name tag said Tamar, so I mentioned the guard.

"I'm always down in there, chasing the fucking raccoons away. They have the fattest raccoons over there. They're like beanbag chairs."

She peered into the carrier.

"How long you had him?"

"About a week or so."

"You're a priest?"

"Yeah. I'm retired."

"You ever been to Israel?"

I told her that I had, but I'd mostly done touristy things.

She was from there, she said. Interested, and also hoping to get in her good graces so she might give Bede a positive verdict, I asked her what'd brought her here.

"The reason's pretty dumb," she said.

She told me she had been born in Tel Aviv. Her grandfather had been a banker, and, as is often the case with the rich, he put a lot of pressure on his son, her father, to achieve something of equal or greater importance in his life. Her father became a lawyer. A mediocre one, she said, because his true passion was not the law, but breaking the law. More specifically, he robbed banks. His motivation was as simple as it sounded.

"He was obvious like that," she said.

But not too obvious—for years she had no knowledge of his motivations or activities, because this life was kept hidden from her throughout her childhood, until one afternoon in the summer of 1991, when he was caught.

"He wasn't the greatest bank robber. He robbed maybe seven banks in twice as many years."

Still, it had been quite the story, as you might imagine: a banker's son turned bank robber. The press couldn't resist, and in this way her father achieved what he'd always wanted, which was to shame his father. Though, of course, this came at the cost of shaming everyone else, especially her, her mother, and her grandmother.

As is the custom when tragedy befalls a family, they sat shiva shortly following the sentencing, since he was effectively dead to them.

"It was around then, while we sulked around the house, that one of my friends gave me a mixtape he'd made. In those long and sad days, I listened to it over and over. The songs were in English, which I didn't know, but the voice was sweet and twirly. I could tell the singer was singing something serious and true. I listened to it for weeks after that. By then, I was embarrassed to ask my friend about it. Then he moved away, and I never got to ask him who it was on the tape."

Soon she learned to play the guitar, and she took her instrument and the tape with her when she joined the army for her two years of obligatory service.

As she spoke, the owl by the desk grew agitated. It started making a barking sound, and flapped its wings against the edges of the cage. Its black eyes locked on the carrier.

Bede started growling and baring his candy-corn teeth through the gap he'd chewed in the door.

"You shut up," Tamar said. The bird turned its massive head toward her and went quiet. So did Bede.

It was there, as a soldier in the army, that she discovered who it was on the cassette. One afternoon, she heard one of the men in her unit listening to a CD, and although she'd never heard the song, she recognized the voice instantly and made him show her the CD case at once.

"It was Dolly Parton," she said. "Do you know her? 'Bargain Store.' I looked at her and her big blond head like she was some kind of angel."

When she returned from her tour of duty, she started a band with two other girls who had just left the armed services. The other two were pretty good musicians, and Tamar had, in her devout copying of Dolly, developed a good singing voice. "But we were punk," she said. Their name translated into something like "emptiness" or "demons." They traveled around for months, playing and partying, until the band broke up and she found herself living off rice and sharing a studio apartment with two other people, one of whom had given her scabies. One afternoon, while sitting at a café and drinking an espresso she'd bought with change stolen from her roommate (he owed her, for the scabies), she heard another song that would change her life. By now, she said, she'd learned a good deal of English—mostly from movies and practicing songs for her band. This song spoke of beautiful mountains, of silver clouds and "starlight . . . softer than a lullaby." She began to cry. It gave her the same feeling Dolly had years ago. She asked the waiter whose song it was, and the waiter told her it was John Denver's "Rocky Mountain High." By now a song was a sign for her. A few days later, she wrote a letter to her grandmother (the banker's widow), and the woman wrote her the check that paid for her plane ticket.

"To Denver," she said. "Land of John Denver. Now I've been here five years."

Paul and I went to Israel in the summer of 1992, just over a decade into my tenure as pastor at St. Antony's. We landed in Tel Aviv and took a bus to the Holy City. A bus full of tourists like us: a trio of rugged nuns, a couple serious families, some very intense Evangelical Christian college students. For four days, we traveled around with this tour group. We swam in the Dead Sea, bobbing in the salty water like boiled eggs (the Evangelical teens wept loudly as they drifted, the cries of abandoned seal pups). We admired the temple wall in our kippahs (the Evangelicals whimpered in steady, funereal shivers). We went to Golgotha and prayed in the Church of the Holy Sepulchre (the teens were inconsolable here, shaking and retching, their faces filled with blood). By the fifth day, we were tired of holy things and Evangelical tears, and so Paul and I broke away from the group and found ourselves in a bar, one with walls covered in pictures of celebrities squeezed next to the same bald, fat man in sunglasses—presumably the owner. One photo, at eye level, showed his rapturous smile as he stood beside a stern Lionel Richie. Since we landed, Paul had been in one of his somber moods, and I thought drinking would help me ride it out. After a while, a man approached our booth. It was the same fat man from the photo, except now, without his sunglasses on, I could see he didn't have any eyebrows. He was completely hairless. He looked like he required a large quantity of milk.

"You two are priests?" he asked in Midwestern American English. "Perfect!" He brought us another round and sat down. He was from Minnesota, it turned out, and had worked for a military contractor neither of us had heard of. "But I've left that behind. I still manage some private security gigs in the region—all really boring stuff. I've branched out." We chatted with him for a while before a woman appeared behind the bar. Upon seeing her, our American friend started nodding at us slowly, as if we were dispensing great wisdom. We'd been talking about sunscreen.

"My wife's a good Catholic girl," he said after she disappeared. "I get in trouble sometimes, so you two are perfect for the optics. Oh, wait! I have something the two of you will just love. Follow me."

He led us to a room in the back and unlocked the door. Behind it was a trove. Autographed photos of Richard Dreyfuss, Whoopi Goldberg, and Billy Crystal, tangles of medals and rosaries, promotional jackets from the previous decade's biggest movies, enough bottles of holy water to quench the thirsts of a dozen parched angels. "Here it is," he said, after fishing through the piles. In his hands was a hand. A thin silver arm crowned with fingers curled in the universal sign of peace. I could see most of it reflected back on our new friend's forehead. "Inside this arm is the arm of St. Agapius."

He passed it around. It was the size of a child's arm, with fingers about as thick as cigarettes.

"Isn't it a little small?" I asked.

"People weren't so big then. Everybody was teensy, because they didn't have any nutrition. Also, I think death shrinks you considerably."

"How did you get this?" Paul asked.

"A client gave it to me as a thank-you gift." He looked

it over. "'I wanna hold your ha-an-and,'" the bald man sang. "'I wanna hold your hand.'"

He stepped out for a minute to scold a bartender, and I inspected the arm a little closer. There was a kind of lid on the back, and without consulting Paul, I unscrewed it. Inside, the arm was hollow. I made Paul peek inside and then screwed it back on as fast as I could.

Our new friend offered to sell it to us, but we politely turned him down. He handed us each a business card and told us, if we ever had any parishioners headed to Israel, he could get them some good deals on tours and relics. Before we left, he asked where we were staying, and then walked outside, hailed a cab, and paid our fare.

"'I wanna hold your hand,'" Paul sang as we climbed in, and then we did for about half a minute, laughing as the taxi drove us back to our hotel. I know this will probably sound strange to you, but we did that sometimes, like children.

I returned to the subject of the coyote.

"Do you think you can take him?"

"Oh, he's been too socialized to humans. We couldn't relocate him. I think we'd have to euthanize."

My distress must have been clear, because she

added: "You should just let him go on your own. There's a state park about five miles west of here. I would just let him out there."

"Can you just take a look at his leg?"

She peeked into the carrier.

"Which one is it?"

"Back right. There should be some gauze on it."

"I don't see any gauze."

He must have chewed it off in the night and left it somewhere in the cemetery.

"I'm not a vet. But he looks okay to me. He's putting weight on it?"

She picked up a rifle from behind the desk.

"I could tranq him if you want."

"No. It's okay."

I picked up the carrier and walked to the door. Before I stepped out, the woman began to sing to herself. It was beautiful. She sounded exactly like Dolly Parton. Or an angel.

※

Shortly after I returned from Israel, Bruno said something to me about my friendship with Paul. We were drinking wine in the basement of some church, just before a dinner with the bishop. Bruno, as I've mentioned, belonged to the neighboring diocese, but he and my bishop were good friends, a fact he reminded me of several times over the course of our conversation. Two embattled conservatives, they stood firm as allies in a war on feminism, liberalism, and any art made after the Reformation. I knew they secretly lusted for a crew-cut authoritarian regime. This had partly been why I was so willing to fill in for him in the past, I understand now, in the hope that he might put in a good word for me.

I mentioned my recent trip to the Holy Land, and Bruno began inquiring about my friendship with Paul (a micro-Inquisition, it seemed to me), sprinkling in a few comments on what he believed to be Paul's unusual preaching style and his memories of Paul as a promising, but ultimately disappointing, student. I deflected, but he pursued. "You and Paul are particularly close, huh?" He elbowed me, gave me a wink, and walked off to chat with some other increasingly inebriated pastor.

"Particularly close." It was a reference to "particular friendship," the close friendships we were all taught to avoid, lest they invite temptation. This was a couple years after the night when the boy had kissed my ring, and about ten years before the story about Bruno broke. In the moment, as I stood there watching the other priests drink and laugh in the basement, I didn't know just what to make of his remarks, but years later I realized what it was: a hint that he had some leverage over me.

Bruno had worn one of the guitar pins that night, a

blue acoustic with a peridot bridge; it looked just like the skull of a jewel-mouthed Cyclops.

※

Just out of the parking lot, I heard Bede's claws tapping against the bottom of the carrier. Once we got close to the park, he started moving around again, bumping his body against the sides of the crate.

I stopped the car by the park to let him out. It maybe wasn't a good idea. But my guess was that he was used to me now. He wouldn't attack me, probably.

I opened the little wire door. He crawled halfway out, stretched his front legs on the seat, and retreated into the carrier.

I would take him as far as Montana, I decided, and let him out there.

21

I charted my route to St. Ignatius. I drove from Fort Collins through Cheyenne, where I stopped for gas and bought dog food and a bag of pretzels. (I had to fish for change in the cup holders. A couple of nickels stuck in the pools of dried coffee at the bottom, like doomed tar-pit mastodons.) From Cheyenne up past Casper and its oil refinery shining in the night like an evil wizard's tower. From Casper through Buffalo, from Buffalo to Sheridan, where I pulled over at a rest stop for a two-hour nap.

I flipped back to the beginning of the *Purple Rain* CD. The stereo was still on the REPEAT setting, replaying the opener over and over through Wyoming's giant clutches of pink rocks. I didn't mind. I liked the metaphysics of it ("Electric word, life / It means forever, and that's a mighty long time . . ."). I thought it might free me from the hold of the title track.

Bruno exerted the pull of a magnetic field or a celestial body. The closer I got to him, the more I could feel him there. At times, it was as if the landscape had reconstituted itself from his body—rocks carved from the hideous pink of his skin, sky extracted from the blue of his eyes, dead trees as blond as his hair—and I was driving over a vast expanse of Bruno-ness.

I had been given a gun. I'd found ammunition. Some signs come delivered by terrifying angels or chatty ghosts, wrapped up in dreams and symbols, and some signs are plain and obvious. They aren't signs at all. They don't signify; they simply are what they are, and you must reckon with them.

Crossing this Brunoan plain, I thought over my plan and its sacramental logic. If I threw the rest of my life away to kill a pedophile priest, maybe I would be somehow absolved of my inaction, my cruelty and willful ignorance toward Paul, my complicity with evil. My evil. Even if not, I would certainly feel better. I'd been carrying Paul, Bruno, my family, and everyone else with me, like a demoniac. It was my fault. I'd been seeking and summoning them in all my idle time. I'd allowed myself to be filled up by the noonday demon, to inflate into a zeppelin of acedia. But somewhere around Sheridan, I drove into a dream. The air around me felt thick and soupy. I ate nuts and chips and dog food. I drove until I had to piss so bad I felt I would die, and then pulled over, rushed out, and, shielded from the road by the car, pissed on some trees. I repeated the slogan off the billboards. Choose life. Choose life. Choose life. I looked at myself in the rearview mirror, and for a moment the man who looked back at me was a stranger. His beard was long and gray. His eyes had dark rings around them. His haggard face was a map of wrinkles that gave way to scrubby hinterlands of beard. He was an old man and a crazy man and a wild man. A prairie wizard, with his own wild dog in the back seat. There were hairs on the end of my nose I'd never noticed before. Long white whiskers.

Bede woke up and started fidgeting in the back seat near Billings. He crawled over the clothes and books, napped in the footwell. After a couple hours, I felt something brush my arm. He'd jumped over the armrest and now sat beside me in the passenger seat. I could smell him.

Somewhere near Nebuchadnezzar, we saw a herd of antelope hopping over a fence. I say "we" because Bede locked in on them. His eyes zagged around, following the arcs of their bounds with menacing curiosity. Then we drove from Nebuchadnezzar through Bozeman, where I passed a yard occupied by an army of a hundred crudely carved wooden bears with the drooping faces of schnauzers. Not long after that, I heard a grinding sound coming from the passenger seat. Bede had found the gun and started gnawing on the handle. I jolted for a moment, before I remembered the bullets were in my pocket. I waited until he grew bored with it and swiped it off the seat.

I should have slept more. A woman at a gas station

in Bozeman recommended I take a frontage road for a while, and in my tired delirium I wound up driving nearly two hours in the wrong direction and spent the next two getting back on course. Furious with the time I'd lost, I kept going until I almost fell asleep at the wheel. This was near Missoula. Luckily, no one was around, and I came to as my tires hit the shoulder. I pulled over and fell asleep as soon as I did. I didn't even coax Bede back into his cage.

When I woke up, a few hours later, I saw little scraps of paper scattered across the car, mâchéd by Bede. My first, horrified thought was that he'd found the letter, but after a frantic fumble through the console I found the grave rubbing, envelope, and paper inside intact. I put the bundle into the glove box so it'd be safe from future attacks.

It was my map Bede had chewed up. Teeth marks perforated the creases, and one corner was damp with slobber. I unfolded it to find a new country, one dotted with mysterious lakes and dark marshlands, everywhere covered with holes.

22

I arrived in St. Ignatius in the evening and stopped at a gas station to prepare myself. Past the lot, the blue Mission Mountains looked like painted fish-teeth. It enraged me that Bruno got to retire in such a beautiful place, even worse that it was named after one of my spiritual heroes.

In the bathroom, I shaved my neck and trimmed my beard with the same pocketknife scissors I'd used to snip the ukulele string. I plucked the hairs off my nose with my fingers and flushed them down. I scrubbed my collar until all the flecks of sauce and coffee were gone, soaked my shirt in the sink, and held it under the hand dryer until it was more or less wearable. Most of the smell went away, and I figured the rest of it would come out once I could get it into a proper washing machine.

I checked myself in the dirty mirror when I was done. The wild man, the prairie wizard, was gone. I looked the part of a priest again.

On my way out, I bought a cheap umbrella. After loading the gun in the car, I tossed the umbrella into the back seat and stuck the gun in its black nylon sleeve.

The rectory was locked. I'd missed my chance to visit him tonight.

It was too cold to sleep in the car. I could have maneuvered my way into a room in the rectory, but I couldn't stomach spending the night in the same building as Bruno. I came up with another plan.

The church was a small, red brick building. The plaque by the steps said it had been built in 1891, though the mission's Jesuit founder had come "at the request of four delegations of Salish and Kootenai" fifty years earlier. As I read, I could hear the building humming liturgically. By the time I walked inside, the Mass was halfway over. I caught a snippet from an uninspired sermon delivered by a priest who was quite obviously a pre–Vatican II type. He preached about obedience, and mentioned a fund-raiser for a ten-year renovation-and-preservation project. A company man. Bruno wasn't there, as far as I could tell.

The ceiling was covered in painted circles of varying sizes, each with a saint or two peeking through, like they were submarine portholes. While the priest rambled on, I stared up at a harp-tickling Cecilia and tried to tune him out.

During the walk back from Communion, I approached one of the confessionals and slipped behind its curtain.

I waited. The small congregation chatted among

themselves and then dispersed. I waited longer. Some-one, probably a janitor, made their rounds. The light went out under the door, and I heard the keys jangle as they locked up.

I waited just a little longer and stepped out.

A church at night is a darkness inside a darkness. I fumbled around, bumping into pews and pillars.

I blindly inched my way along until I remembered the lighter in my pocket.

In the light of its fat orange flame I could see the empty pews, the stations of the cross, the statues of saints rendered reaperlike in the shadows. At St. Antony's, after we pulled back from our Haiti missions, the par-ish council proposed we seriously renovate our worship space. Over the course of the next year or so, they raised the three hundred thousand dollars necessary to enlarge the nave, add a chapel, and rebuild the altar.

I didn't like the renovations. I missed the simplicity of our old space. For weeks, I gave sermons with little jabs at the improvements. I never felt I could honestly say what I was feeling back then. I think that is what hap-pens when you live inside a church. You let in the light, but the glass is tinted. You only get some of it. You don't get it all until you leave.

Once I felt enough time had passed, I unlocked the church door and went out to the car to get my things.

When I first imagined I'd sleep in the church, I figured I'd leave the coyote in the car. But now that the sun had gone down, it was much too cold. I brought the carrier in with me, along with the derringer, Paul's letter, and the rest of my supplies. I set up camp in the chapel, an alcove crowded with a couple Marys, a spare Christ, and a statue of a Jesuit, presumably the mission's founder. The altar, with its rug, would have been more comfortable, but I haven't lost all respect for sanctuary. I set the envelope on the plinth, between the priest's sandals, then took ten votive candles from the shrine, lit them, and set them here and there around me. I pissed in the bucket under the Jesuit's watchful eyes. (I was careful not to get any on the floor, but if I did, so what?) I set the derringer next to the letter on the plinth and looked into the eyeholes of the skull on the handle.

I opened two cans of tuna and unlatched the carrier door to feed Bede. I realized I'd left the water jug in the car, and went to get it.

When I returned, the carrier was open. Bede was gone.

I patrolled the nave. I ambled the ambulatory. I circled the altar like a druid.

The coyote had the upper hand. Every pew was its own trench, its own gully in which to hide. He had the cover of the pulpit and could easily stow himself behind the aisle-facing pews that lined the skinny ambulatory. I saw no trace of him.

I couldn't turn the lights on for fear someone outside might see it. Instead, I grabbed more candles from the shrine and dropped them every few feet up and down the aisles, lighting each of them until their soft orange glow blanketed the lowest ten feet of the church. The upper reaches were still perfectly black.

With the church thus illuminated, I made another patrol. I checked the narthex. I crossed the transept. On a hunch, I returned to the altar and pulled back the cloth.

Underneath I found a pile of hymnals, many with pages torn out and shredded up. A couple covers, I noticed, had little lanes scratched into them. Teeth marks.

Having routed him from his den, I doubled back through the aisle. This time I glimpsed his shadow in the ambulatory. Cast against the light on the wall, I saw the silhouette of a black wolf the size of a dumpster.

I pursued him, chasing the shadow, but lost my quarry somewhere in the chapel.

It went on like this for a while. I caught his eyes shining down a pew across the aisle. I heard his claws clack near the organ. I flushed him from the sacristy, only to lose him all over again in the nave.

I gave up. Just before I blew out the candles, I took a

look at the altar. What I'd mistaken for the few set-piece scenes from Jesus's life were, I saw, paintings of Ignatius's three visions. In each, the saint stared up at the God-head like a teen at a concert. At first, I was struck by the panels' beauty, but then something began to bother me, beyond the fact that Bruno had worshipped, perhaps even celebrated the Mass, in front of them. Everyone in the mural—Jesus, Mary, Ignatius—was sickly pale, in European dress. It was a mirror for the priests to admire themselves in. This was why I'd always kept my worship space spare. You wind up making God in your own image and forget to look for Him anywhere else. I gathered up the votive candles and blew them out like I was having a lonely birthday, saving one so I could find my way back to where I'd set my sleeping bag.

I lay there on the floor for a while with the red candle on my chest, staring up at the saints in their port-holes and waiting for the sound of Bede's claws on the tile, until I fell asleep.

That night, I had a very troubling dream. In it, I was laid out on the ground with my wrists and ankles tied. I was either an ancient martyr or a soul in Hell. My back stung—I'd been set on a bed of thorns—and as I tried to get up, the ropes only tightened, pressing me back to the needles with even greater pressure. In a brief moment of slack, I managed to get myself up and turned my head to see the implements of my torture. There, spread out on the ground of my dreams, were hundreds of lapel pins, a forest of metal spikes and the oblong outlines of guitars.

I woke up the next morning to find I'd grabbed the derringer in my sleep. My hand was sore from squeezing it so tight. The safety, I discovered in terror, was off.

Bede was back in his carrier, passed out. I shut the door and quickly packed up. I left the nest of hymnals and candles on the floor. I wonder what they made of that.

23

That morning, before I snuck out of the church and made my way to Bruno, I rewetted my hair in the baptismal font and checked my reflection in the water. I didn't smell too good, but I didn't think anyone would notice that. I stuck Paul's letter in my jacket pocket and put the gun back in the nylon umbrella sleeve. Tucked under the arm, it looked natural enough, if a little crooked.

In my preparations to confront Bruno, I'd forgotten to arrange to finally let Bede go. Not far from the church was a skate park and a blanched little wood, the edges of which were littered with cigarette butts and at least two decaying Wendy's bags. I parked at the very edge of the gravel lot opposite the park and opened the car door, then the wire door to Bede's carrier. Bede was still asleep inside. I left the doors open for him, to get out in his own time.

In the lobby, an elderly secretary directed me down the hall, to a second building, attached by a corridor with big windows that showed off a row of dead bushes and a chalky Virgin Mary.

I passed rooms of frail and withered priests with their walkers and wheelchairs. Terrible paintings hung on the wall, evidently the work of deranged children.

In one, a crude angel shepherded colored blobs that might have been the souls of the faithful on their way to Heaven, perhaps the very souls of these ancient priests. It was the kind of place where I'd thought I might very well end up, since I have no close family to take me in, and as I walked the halls, I took some comfort in knowing that, when I was done in Bruno's room, I'd prefer prison to this anyway.

A young seminarian, in his black dress of a cassock, shoved a marooned walker aside and approached me.

"Could you help me find Father Bruno?"

"He's the last one on the left. I'll take you to him. Old friends?"

"Pretty old, yeah."

"Nice umbrella," he said, scanning the butt of the gun. "Memento mori, am I right?"

He led me to a room at the end of the hall.

"It's nice of you to come. He doesn't get many visitors. I don't know if you're up to date on his condition, but don't get too down if he doesn't recognize you. It'll do him good just to feel your presence."

"It's been a while anyway. Just want to check in, you know."

"You cold? Your hands are shaking."

"I'm just old."

The room was small and simply furnished. A bed, two chairs, a TV mounted high on the wall next to a framed photograph of the last pope to make the great refusal. A big window looking out over what I hoped wasn't a parochial school.

Bruno was ten years older than me—a negligible amount when I was forty or fifty, but twenty years later that extra decade had set him, if not on death's door, then at least on his stoop. He was tiny. His skin looked like it had been skimmed off old pudding, and his ears were small and bloodless, hanging from his head like two pale tea bags. Bruno's famously fat head had deflated, like an old balloon, and the extra flesh drooped into jowls. Underneath all that skin and jowl, he had the skull of a cat.

"James," I said, shaking him awake. "James. Do you remember me? Dan. From St. Antony's?"

He looked at me blankly. Some dried-up drool frosted his chin.

I slid the gun out of its sleeve and popped the stubborn nub of the safety. I thought I could pull him out of his feigned stupor.

A gentle knock on the door. I shoved the gun back into the black sleeve as fast as I could.

"Father James?"

The door opened, and a young man's head poked through.

"Sorry to interrupt your visit. Just stopping by to

bring James Communion. He's the last one to get it. I'll be quick."

He was a priest, too, though he looked even younger than the seminarian. He was a bit overweight, with pale skin that made him look like a giant baby, full of milk.

"Oh man. It doesn't smell too good in here. A skunk must've come by the window. That happens sometimes."

I didn't get the chance to turn the safety back on before I'd shoved the gun into the umbrella case. I tried to press it through the nylon, but I was afraid I might accidentally pull the trigger. I was still awkwardly holding the black bundle in my hands. I set it gently under one of the chairs by the nightstand and prayed it wouldn't go off.

The young priest started in on the blessing as he dragged a chair between us and sat down. He pulled the host out of a pyx, the golden pocket-mirror of a box we use to deliver the sacrament to the sick. The lid showed a priest in the middle of the consecration, hoisting the bread to Heaven, with the figure's head eerily obscured by the host. A bread-headed man.

With his plump marshmallow hands, the young priest split the host in two and held one half out to Bruno, who lurched forward and took it on his tongue like a trained dolphin. The priest placed the other half in my hands, and I ate it.

"I'll let you two get back to your visit," he said when he was done.

As I stood up to walk him to the door, my foot touched the derringer, and I made a frantic, jerky hop away from the weapon. The young priest grabbed my arm and helped me back into the chair.

"You sit, now. God bless you both." Then, in a much louder voice, as if shouting to an upstairs neighbor, "SEE YOU NEXT SUNDAY, JAMES!"

He gave the rapist a brilliant smile, touched one of his shriveled hands, and left.

I waited a few seconds, then shut the door and pulled the gun back out of its sleeve. My stomach gurgled—the host was the first thing I'd eaten all day. I turned the safety back on and wiped my sweaty palm on my pants.

The derringer seemed much too light now, as if the whole thing was hollow. The barrel was comically short, and it occurred to me that I could snap the bone handle with my bare hands if I tried. I wished I'd found a more substantial implement, something I could anchor myself to. It felt like the gun and I, at the mere suggestion of a breeze, could be swept down the hall, past the other dying priests, out the door, and up into the sky like one of the disturbed children's metaphysical crayon blobs.

Bruno kept his hands churched on the ghost of his paunch and stared up at the black TV screen. He didn't notice the gun. I aimed the derringer right at him, but he didn't react.

I stuck it in his face. The bone of the handle looked as if it had popped out of my arm. The nubs at the end had somehow managed to slip under the ukulele string on my wrist.

He regarded it blankly, as if I were offering him some foreign food.

I popped the stub of the safety out of place. He still didn't move. I opened his mouth and put the barrel on his tongue like it was the host. Nothing.

Above his bed, the crucified Jesus stared down at me. He had an impossible number of abs. They multiplied like loaves. I couldn't absolve myself with someone else's blood. I couldn't erase my own sin with another sin. I had long missed my chance to do right, and now I was here, trying to kill the dead.

I threw up in the trash can and wrapped the gun back up in its miniature cassock, and God was very far away.

On my way out, I noticed something on his nightstand. The box of pins. Inside, a hoard of miniature guitars gleamed back at me.

"How was it?" the seminarian asked me in the hallway. "Hope you had a good visit."

"I did. He gave me these." I rattled the box.

"His pins? He loves those. Wow. You must have been close."

"Yeah."

I should have sold them, and donated the money to some worthy cause. Instead, I threw them in the dumpster in the parking lot.

24

I drove through the cork-colored plains of eastern Washington.

When I returned to the car, I'd found Bede still inside, asleep. I shut him back in, telling myself I'd find him a better home. The Mission Mountains were beautiful, but I needed to leave him somewhere far away from Bruno. It was my last excuse to put off freeing him.

Somewhere near Moses Lake, the sun went down and the sky turned purple-black. I felt like I was driving across the surface of the moon. A couple hours later, we crossed into western Washington, through a wall of lanky pines and shaggy hemlocks.

I pulled over to the side of the road, not far off the highway. When I got out, I could still hear the cars speeding by, and, given Bede's history with the interstate, I decided to drive a little farther.

I followed a county road and pulled off where a bridge crossed a stream. While I was at it, I thought, I might as well get rid of the gun, too, so I stuck it in my jeans. Bede was asleep in the carrier. I checked the latch on the door and took him down the slope of the bank.

The surface of the water looked like it'd been hammered out of pink tin. The trees leaned over, admiring their reflections in the stream. Ferns on the bank faced the water, fanning out into green stars. You could hear the stream murmur to itself as it flowed by. It was the kind of place I would like to vanish into.

I opened the crate, and Bede stepped out. His ears moved like moth wings as he sniffed the air. He walked over to the water and took a drink. His back leg looked strong. He was putting his weight on it. I knew he would be okay.

The water carried a frond past his muzzle as he drank. I made the sign of the cross over the stream. I scooped some water up in my hands and sprinkled it on Bede and blessed him. I reached into the water again and blessed myself, then the gun, which I figured I'd drop into the water while I was here. There were hatch marks near the skull from where Bede had gotten hold of it.

This would be the last I'd see of Bede, I told myself, and looked him over so I could remember him. His back looked like an overgrown wheat field, a tiny savanna starting at the lowlands of his neck. His ears were pulled back as he bent over the stream. He was drinking a lot. I could hear his tongue smack against the surface of the water. I reached out to pat his head.

He jerked around and bit me. Like a creature from a sermon. His teeth went deep into the meat of my hand, then caught on the ukulele string as he pulled away.

"Fuck!" I shouted, and then the coyote, whom I'd named but who in truth had no name, took off up the slope of the bank.

I left the carrier behind. With my unbitten hand I grabbed the gun and went after him. I should have just let him go, but the pain and shock of the bite filled me with rage. I wanted to catch him and kick him and kill him.

When I was just a couple yards behind, I aimed the gun at him and fired.

Nothing happened. Not to Bede, anyway. The kickback on the derringer was so strong I thought it might have broken my unbitten hand.

Bede stayed along the road, and I followed in full sprint. My knee started clicking in even, metronomic intervals, hurting a little more with each stride. Occasionally, Bede turned his head and I glimpsed the glowing orbs of his eyes. We ran through the trees, over the leaves and stones just beyond the shoulder. The moon was the color of an apricot. For a minute there, I wasn't chasing him, but running with him, part of the same dark thing as him.

But not really. We came to a fence. The coyote crouched for a moment and looked at me. Then he sprang up, drew his legs to chest, and in one balletic leap crossed the wire and bounded through the brush on the other side. I caught one last look at his tail as he slipped into the darkness.

I began my long walk back to the car. My legs and back ached. My hand was bleeding badly, and a lot of the blood had dripped onto my jeans, jacket, and the gun. Later, when I made it back to the car, I'd pour hydrogen peroxide on it and wrap it in the same gauze I'd used on the coyote. Only then did I see just where his teeth had sunk in—right in the middle of my palm. A half-assed stigmata.

25

In the morning, I called Clara and left a message telling her I'd be there by evening.

After I freed Bede, I stopped at a hospital outside Seattle and they put seven stitches in my hand. I told the doctor about my medications and medical history, and she gave me a prescription for antibiotics.

Because my injuries weren't too great, and because I'd dressed the wound pretty well myself, I sat in the waiting room for two hours before they saw to me.

To my left sat a man with an arrow in his leg. It stuck out of him like a porcupine quill.

"My son did it," he said to me when he saw I was staring. "My wife and him and I were bow hunting and he thought I was a deer. It's not too deep. I wanted to pull it out myself, but she wouldn't have it."

He flapped the *National Geographic* he'd been reading toward a woman dozing on the chair beside him.

"What happened to you?" he asked me.

I told him I'd been bitten by a coyote.

"They don't usually attack people, far as I know."

"I thought it was a dog."

"You should never touch a wild animal. That's why

they call them wild animals. I saw a show about a guy who worked at an ape sanctuary where they had all these TV monkeys. One day, one of the chimps got out and ripped the guy's arms off and beat him to death with them. With his own arms, like nunchucks. I suppose he was probably already mostly dying once his arms came off, but it was pretty clear that you shouldn't mess with a wild thing. Stories like that stick with you. Apparently, the chimp had been on TV several times, mostly on cop shows and sitcoms. I think he'd been on *Hawaii Five-0*. Of course, a son isn't much better than a chimpanzee. I guess every kid wants to kill their parents on some level, at some point or another. Oedipal Rex."

The woman lying beside him perked up. She'd been listening in.

"What are you talking about? You shot your own self."

"You caught me," he said, and laughed. "I was setting up a remote-control crossbow. So I could shoot things when I'm at work. Via webcam. I have a salt lick set up and put a camera out there."

"Jay—that's our son—he doesn't hunt," his wife said. "He's against it. He thinks the accident's fate coming down on us."

"It's just kind of embarrassing, I guess," the man said.

The arrow in his leg had fins on the end that looked

like guitar picks. The shaft was covered in a leopard-print pattern.

Half an hour later, a nurse walked toward us and announced his name.

"This is me," he said. I watched the arrow in his leg whip around like a conductor's baton as he and his wife walked off.

I got to Seattle four hours before I told Clara I'd be there. I found their neighborhood on the map and parked my car a few blocks away from where they lived, hoping to kill the last few hours walking around the neighborhood and show up on time.

The Camry smelled like wet mulch, mildewed towels, dead moss, roadkill, wood smoke, and maybe a little kerosene. I stepped out of the stench like a diver yanking himself from the undertow.

I walked past a grade school, a community college, and a park. I told myself not to forget to check on Bede, before I remembered he was gone. Since I let him go, my mind kept wandering to him, as if he was still in my car and had to be fed or sedated.

As I walked around, the mountain in the distance seemed to listen in and watch me from its periphery. My bitten hand felt fine under the gauze, but the other one, the one I'd used to fire the derringer, throbbed like it had its own heart and lungs.

An hour went by like this, and then I couldn't resist the urge to see my friends any longer. Surely they'd find it ridiculous, that I'd been circling the block, waiting to see them.

I pulled my car in front of the mailbox.

The house didn't have any corners—it was a perfect cylinder, and could have been computer-animated. In the middle was a cyclopic window about the size of a hot tub.

I rang the doorbell. Brian answered. He was more bald than when I last saw him, eight or nine years ago.

"Dan! You're early! Come on in!"

I detected some irritation in his voice, but then he drew me in for a hug and led me into the house.

"Clara! Dan's here!"

We passed a row of framed prints of medieval woodcuts, a photograph of a convent from our trip to Mexico years ago, and an illumination by Hildegard of Bingen. I know that last one, because I gave it to them.

In between these were pictures of Brian. Brian talking with his hands while men in fleece vests stood in rapt attention; Brian smiling beside a couple Buddhist monks decked out in wine-colored robes; Brian onstage in some vast theater, wearing a headset microphone, with the word "creativity" projected on the screen behind him.

We found Clara in the kitchen, unloading the dishwasher. She was shorter than I remembered. She looked like she had been distilled. Her edges were sharper. I don't know what that means, exactly, but that was the impression. She wore a pair of round yellow glasses that took up most of her face.

"Hey!" She came over and hugged me. "You're a little early. Ooh, I'm liking this new beard. Very prophetic." Her Mexican accent was less noticeable than I remembered. "What the fuck happened to your hand?"

"I found a dog on the side of the road that had been hit by a van."

Clara: "And it bit you?"

"Not right away. I put it in my car and tried to get it to a vet."

Brian pulled a tray of vegetables out of the refrigerator. The two of them looked so trim and healthy, they could have been yoga instructors, or Mormons. Brian's cheekbones had surfaced, and I could see all the little muscles in Clara's face as she chewed on a carrot. Suddenly I had the urge to get out of there, to run to my car and drive to Los Angeles or Florida, or even Boston. "Actually, it was a coyote."

Clara: "You put a fucking coyote in your car?"

"It was kind of dazed."

Brian: "So it came out of it and bit you?"

"No. I had him for a couple of days. I let him out near some place called Whittier. The leg had healed pretty well."

Clara: "You drove a coyote all the way from Indiana?"

"I found him in Illinois."

Clara: "Jesus, Dan." I caught the end of a glance over to Brian, a quick twitch of her eyebrow. "I can't say I'm surprised."

I tried to change the subject.

"What about you guys? How have you two been?"

Brian: "We're good. I mean, as good as you can be right now, in this country."

"We're doing really well, though," Clara said. "Brian has been doing a lot of creative consulting for the technocrats. He's kind of a guru now."

Brian: "I just want to help people make things." He stared nobly through the huge window so this could sink in. "When our company sold, I had a little time for the first time since college, really, so I went deep into creativity studies. Now I mostly do guided sessions, light hypnosis. Clara made me do the Spiritual Exercises not long after we got here—it's really not so different."

It's different.

"He's helped me out of a few creative binds," Clara said through a mouthful of celery. "You should let him do a session with you."

"I saw the pictures when we came in," I said. "You look like a rock star." A little condescension leaked through my voice, I'll admit. Brian was never really my favorite.

Brian: "And Clara just had her big show, so . . ."

"Oh, really? When was that?"

Clara: "Want some hummus?"

"Sure," I said. "Thanks."

"Two weeks ago. You said you were going to try and make it."

"Oh. Yeah. I'm sorry."

Clara dropped some coffee mugs into the sink.

"Dan, it's just . . . it's hard to be your friend sometimes. We love you. We really meant it when we said we wanted you to visit us out here. I really wanted you to see my show! You were a big part of my inspiration! But then you don't come. And then you do come, but with only one day's notice. And now you're early, and you show up smelling like dog shit and looking like you haven't slept in a week."

There was another print in the kitchen—it looked like a page from a book of hours. Laborers, dressed in blue and red, toiled in the fields before a vast white castle. A giant wall sat between them and the castle.

"I'm sorry."

"I never thought of our friendship in a tit-for-tat kind of way. But we were so close! And then we never saw you, except for that time we came to you. In Indiana! We live by the Pacific Ocean! Surrounded by forests! And mountain ranges! And you're retired!" She looked over to Brian again. I had the sense they'd talked about what she was going to say to me. "It hurt my feelings. You could have been out here with us, and instead you were back there."

"They let me go."

Brian: "What? Why?"

"The bishop told me to go. He said I had to leave and I could go wherever I wanted."

Clara: "But *why?*"

"We have a lot of bad history. Remember when he heard about the funeral of the king of the Gypsies?"

Brian: "I think it's 'Roma.' Yeah."

"And I think he figured out about Paul being gay. So he's had it out for me."

Clara: "How is Paul? Did you two ever get back in touch?"

"No. He died."

Brian: "I'm sorry."

He'd waxed his head so it shone like a Christmas ornament. I could see the pale shades of me and Clara in the pink world of it.

Clara: "But you still haven't told us why you left."

"We used to have these vegetable gardens and flower beds from when the place was a parish school," I told them. "But they all went to weeds. And since I was leading retreats there, I thought I could make something out of it. I made a project of cleaning it up. I thought I'd make it into a little Zen garden."

Clara: "I always loved those weird projects. That labyrinth you always used to bring out. I loved that. But go on."

"Thanks." I drew a cartoon eyeball in the hummus with a carrot. I left it poked in there when I was done. "I went around the grounds and found a bunch of big rocks. I pulled the weeds and dug a few inches down so I could lay some bricks for a base. I bought some pea gravel from Lowe's. I made a rake out of dowel rods and a scrub brush. I thought it was really cool. I raked a pattern into it that I saw in a book.

"Not long after I finished, a deacon asked what it was and I explained it to him. I thought he'd be into it. I really thought, *He's a young guy, he'd like it.* But when I was finished telling him about it, I saw he was terrified. And when the bishop called the next day, I knew what was happening."

Clara: "I don't see how that's bad. Out here they'd have no problem with something like that."

Brian: "Fuck. I'm going to call our bishop. Or write a letter to the cardinal. Pope Francis wouldn't stand for that shit. You gave your whole life to those fuckers."

"It's a conservative diocese."

Clara: "I can't believe it. After all these years, they just let you go. So where did they send you?"

"Nowhere. I mean, I still get a pension. But they don't have anywhere to send me."

"You didn't fight them on that? There are a lot of places you could go. Why didn't you push back?"

Me: "I don't like those old fathers' homes anyway."

Clara: "You shouldn't've rolled over like that."

Brian: "So where have you been living?"

"I've been staying in my car. I know that sounds crazy, but actually it's been pretty fun. Driving around."

Brian: "Jesus, man."

Clara: "You can stay with us as long as you like. I don't know why you wanted to stay around in Indiana. We've always wanted you to move out here!"

Something had shifted. I'd maneuvered out of her interrogation.

"You don't have to take care of me."

Clara: "It's not a burden! We love you, you fucking weirdo."

She opened a bottle of wine, and we started talking about other things, reminiscing about the old parish and the prime of our friendship.

"Do you remember that nurse?" I asked after a couple drinks. "The one who moved to Haiti?"

"I couldn't stand that bitch," Clara said. "We always

just called her 'Haiti.'" She folded her hands, tilted her head, and agonized her brows into a little holy-card face, à la St. Agnes. "Do you know if she made it out of the earthquake okay?"

"I don't. I don't know."

Clara: "Have you been working on anything lately?"

"No, not really. I haven't been feeling too inspired."

"Brian could do one of his sessions on you. I'll do it, too! Brian, let's do it. Please?"

Brian and I looked at each other and nodded. We knew better than to refuse her. Clara was relentless. Twice back in Muncie, when the two of us were locked out on their third-story balcony, I'd seen her punch through a glass sliding door, laughing as she picked the glass out of her knuckle and licked off the blood like spilled jelly. The second time, it turned out the door had merely jammed, but she was so eager to punch through it again that she didn't double-check.

"All right," Brian said, and had us sit down on the carpet in front of the living-room couch. Clara and I had our necks against the cushion. Brian sat between and behind us, on the couch itself. He put his hand on my shoulder.

"I want you to picture a place where you feel most creative. The place where you're most comfortable. Most at home. Don't think about it in your head, but locate it in your heart, from a place of gratitude. Now I want you to picture this home-place, where you sit, what the light looks like coming through the window."

I tried to envision the kind of place he described, but I couldn't come up with anything. He continued the session with something about "compassionate mentors" and our innate "child wisdom," but by then I'd given up. I kept my eyes open and looked around at their beautiful house full of books, pictures, and light.

At some point, after we'd had a few more drinks, Clara got up and said she wanted to show me something. She led me out of the house and into a hut in the backyard that she'd fashioned into a studio.

"I've been working on this series about *The Cloud of Unknowing*. That was part of what my show was about. I thought you might like it. Anyway, I want to say that the exercises meant a lot to me. They still mean a lot to me."

Most of her paintings looked like murky bags of bugs and fish, crawling or swimming between deep holes. I loved them, and told her so.

"Thanks. Thank you."

In one, a creature—it might have been a centipede— skulked behind a diaphanous rotting leaf.

"How are you really doing?" Clara asked as I studied the paintings.

"I'm good. It's been pretty peaceful since I left the rectory. And it was really nice to see Paul's husband,

Tim. I feel like I can really live in the present out on the road. It's my way of imitating the Desert Fathers. Did I ever lend you the *Sayings*?"

I could feel her looking at me. I asked her about the holes in the paintings.

"I know your tricks, Dan. You'll give a homily about pretty much anything before you tell me how you feel. Or you make other people do all the work. You ask them questions, get them talking, and then you can vanish. Then you have their story to hide inside of, whenever you need it. You're doing it right now."

She wasn't wrong, but there was nothing I could say that would make her feel any better. She wound up answering my question about the holes anyway.

"It was something that came up in the exercises. You told me about apophasis. The via negativa. Your migraines. I think about that shit all the time. You know, when Brian first tried that exercise on me, I thought of you—as one of my compassionate mentors. You, Helen Frankenthaler, and David Bowie."

I told her about the bottomless pit in Kansas and the girl I almost took with me.

"You were really going to bring her here?"

"I thought so."

"Wow. I guess I always thought you were good with kids. But I'm surprised you were willing to go through with things."

"What do you mean?"

"I've never known you to commit to things like that."

"I've been a priest since 1973. I committed to that."

"I guess to people is what I mean. It's one of the things that makes it hard to be friends with you. We get close, and then you disappear. I get the feeling that you could just drop me at any point and just be fine. I mean, you have. You did it with Paul, too."

I didn't have anything to say to that, either.

"All I'm saying is that it feels that way. You're like a cat. You're slippery." She stuck up her hands, like a bank robber giving up. "I'm not trying to litigate things. I'm glad you're here."

She straightened a stack of books on her desk. I saw a copy of *The Cloud of Unknowing* in there—I'd given it to her before she moved.

"I'll have to go see that bottomless pit someday."

She rearranged her brushes and pens in their reused yogurt containers. I looked at the paintings and drawings for a while, until Brian called for us and we went back to the house.

The next morning, we drove out to Mount Rainier. We'd decided on it the night before, when we were drunk. It still sounded like a good idea when we woke up, so we climbed into their station wagon and left. We took a road aimed straight toward the mountain, so that the whole way the snowy peak was right in front of us, taking up more and more of the windshield. "There are bears up there," Brian said. "There are mountain lions on the mountain, too. Mountain-mountain lions. But they're all afraid of people. Understandable."

We passed a ranger booth and parked near the trailhead. By now all the trees were different. They were thicker and older, with orange bark. These were the same trees that flanked us as we set off on the trail. Clara gave me a walking stick, which helped me keep my balance on the incline and switchbacks, though I had to brace it with my sore hand, since the other was still wrapped up. We walked by young men and women with heavy backpacks and scruffy dogs, some of which had their own little backpacks. We passed old couples walking with ski poles, like Nordic explorers. We stood by an enormous waterfall—the runoff from an ancient mountain glacier, Brian explained. We went higher and came to an alpine meadow of red-and-purple wildflowers that, to me, looked like a dream that had spilled out of some poet's head. I scanned the trees at every turn. I thought of Bede, who was surely more than a hundred miles away. We went higher and spotted a marmot darting across the rocks. The trail thinned to a tread no wider than a Bible. I forgot about the wound on my hand entirely. Above us, a flock of white birds circled upward on a thermal, tracing the shape of the air.

We went even higher and came to a mountain stream. This was around the fourth hour or so. We decided to rest there. Brian and Clara laid out their backpacks, and we ate some oranges on the rocks at the edge of the water.

"Did you hear that?" Brian asked. "Listen."

We sat there in the quiet. A loud crack echoed from somewhere inside the mountain.

"It's ice, breaking off. Glacial ice." He said it was why we couldn't drink the water. Because of ancient bacteria waking up in the sunlight. Resurrecting.

Brian picked up the orange peels and stuck them in his backpack. Clara took off her shoes and stuck her bare feet in the water. They were angels in repose. I felt a thousand miles away from civilization and man-made things. I was an animal held in place by the water, grass, and mountain. I looked at Brian and Clara and the water and the mountain and I loved them. Even Brian. It was a kind of Heaven, or it was Heaven. My whole body was praying. I was starting to feel a little better about my Montana detour.

When they weren't looking, I pulled the derringer out of my bag and dropped it into the water. I mouthed a quick blessing as it sank into the stream.

We went higher. Brian gave me his binoculars and I watched an eagle fly over a rocky peak. Then we decided we'd gone far enough and turned around to retrace our path. What took us five hours to climb only took three hours to descend. Halfway down, we picked up a little speed, until Clara and Brian were bounding like deer far ahead of me, leaping over the rocks and roots along the path. Occasionally, they stopped and waited for me to catch up. (I'm too old to run like that. My legs and back still hurt from chasing Bede. The nights in the car were catching up to me.) We'd walk together for a while, until they gradually regained speed, and we did the whole thing all over again.

We stopped to watch the waterfall at twilight. I took off my jacket, and something fell to the ground.

It was the spoon, the white plastic spoon I'd been feeding Bede with. There was still some Spam on it, hard and purple in its little bowl. I checked my coat and discovered a kidney-shaped blotch where it had stuck to the denim like a leech.

I picked the spoon off the rocks and put it in my pocket.

The night we came back from the mountain, I had a strange dream, much stranger than the pin dream. They were two dreams, really. Two that I remember, though it feels like I raced through a hundred dreams and instantly forgot them. In the first, I was standing on the ball of paint like it was the whole world. I just walked around for a while, and every now and then it changed color, like a mood ring, and that was it. In the second dream, I was sitting on a giant king- or queen-sized bed. My parents were on the bed with me, except they were babies, just a few months old, with big eyes, and fat hands like mini-muffins. My brothers and sisters were babies, too. So were Paul, Clara, and Anna. I was myself, the way I am now, sitting there, surrounded by the babies. I picked them up and held them. I made sure they didn't crawl too close to the edge of the bed. I wrapped them up in blankets and sang to them until they fell asleep. I was their father and son both, and brother, and mother, and it was my job to sit there and take care of them and make sure nothing bad ever happened to them. And then I woke up in Brian and Clara's guest room and prayed I might fall back asleep, into the same dream.

After lying there for a while, I felt a sudden panic. I was convinced I'd lost Paul's letter. I rooted through all my things, dumping out my duffel bag on the floor. The letter and grave rubbing were still in my pocket, it turned out—in my terror, I'd searched poorly.

Already the envelope was showing signs of wear. I went into the kitchen and looked through the drawers until I found a Ziploc freezer bag. I put the letter and rubbing inside and double-checked the seal until I was sure they were safe, completely incorruptible.

On the ride back home from the mountain, they offered again to let me stay with them.

Clara: "We talked about it last night, before we went to bed. We have the mother-in-law apartment. You could stay in there. We were thinking about renting it out, but we'd rather have you."

"Wow. Thanks."

"I've been wanting to move my studio space into the house so I don't have to go back and forth so much."

Out the window, I saw the dome of an enormous stadium, shining like a fat white boil.

"Is it okay if I think about it for a day?"

"Of course."

I could tell I'd disappointed her. But it was a big decision. Who could blame me for wanting to think about it?

Brian turned the radio on, and we listened to someone talk about the impending nuclear standoff and an upcoming television show about a struggling stand-up comedian created by a stand-up comedian.

I turned around and watched the mountain shrink behind us. Even after hours of driving, it never got small enough to ignore.

26

It was an evening like all the other evenings that summer. A Friday in August, at our house in Fort Wayne. I was eleven. I'd spent the day riding bikes with my friends around the neighborhood. I don't remember much of that, aside from a ride down to the quarry, which was mostly full of water, leaving only a thin ring of stone around the vast pool. A dog had been running laps around the ring, looking for a way out. He was so skinny we couldn't decide if he was a greyhound or just starving. My brother took a piece of bread out of his pocket, wadded it into a ball, and rolled it down to him, and this made us feel better.

I don't remember much of dinner, either, but right after, I went to my room, a room I shared with three of my brothers. I felt sick and lay down. I began to sweat, and so I took off all my clothes and lay in bed until I fell asleep.

When I woke up a few hours later, the house was completely dark. And quiet. A rare thing in my family of a dozen people. Apparently, everyone either had a date or a party to go to, including my parents, and I'd been left behind in the chaos of their makeup, showers, hair spray, and cologne. Our house was never empty or quiet. Every corner teemed with life, like a pet shop. Someone was always listening to the radio or arguing about 45s or running a bath or making a sandwich or trying to eat the last chip, carrot, or pretzel without anyone else's noticing.

I got up and walked through the silent house, passing from room to room like a ghost in my bare feet. I couldn't see anything. I reached for the light switch, but nothing happened when I flipped it. I felt for the matchbox in the cupboard and found my mother's devotional Mary candle, which I lit to guide me through the house.

No light came in from outside. The windows looked like they'd been painted black. The rooms were mysterious to me. The table and chairs were unfamiliar, as if they'd been secretly replaced by slightly different models. The pictures on the wall could've been of anybody. The Virgin's face flickered in my hand. She wore her fiery heart on her chest, a meaty brooch.

As I stood there, in the glow of the Mary candle, the whole world was the house. A dim box surrounded by a viscous, rolling darkness. There had to be another life beyond the one I had there and then, I knew. I could just barely feel the signs of it, whatever it was, swirling in corners of my eyes, brushing up against the hairs of my arms. I wanted to call out to someone and make them feel this with me, or shout out to whatever it was around me. But I knew it was like a rabbit or a bird, would dart off if I moved even just a little.

Outside, I heard some animal shaking the bushes. The sound was like someone stepping on a bag of potato chips. I had the sense it was just the two of us, that animal and me, in the whole world. It was the thing I was feeling concentrated into a body, and I wanted to see what it looked like.

I stepped outside, only to hear the sound of it scampering around the corner of the house.

That was when I saw that all the lights in the neighborhood had gone dark. The moon was a flake of cereal, or skin. Not a single light from the window of any house could be seen.

I heard the animal again, moaning. Calling out to its mate, or dying. I followed the sound to my backyard, through the trees, the next few yards, and into the woods beyond the neighborhood.

I followed it down to the quarry. I lost the sound. The animal disappeared. I decided I would climb down and look at the water, which appeared to me to be a pool of absolute blackness.

In daylight, the quarry was inscribed with beautiful blue rings, two or three layers, each about three feet thick, that wound unbroken around the top of the pit. Now it was a vast black crater, God's inkwell, though I thought I could still see some of the blue in the moonlight.

The slope was soft enough that I could edge my way down, and after a while I made it to the lowest tier, where we'd seen the dog earlier. I thought this animal might be the dog, but it was nowhere in sight. I listened to the water splash against the stone. I stuck one of my feet in, and then I jumped.

The icy water swallowed me. I was, at this point, still naked, and the cold water sucked the last of the warmth out of my body. I paddled up, toward the moon, and when I surfaced I resolved to cross the pool.

It took me about half an hour. I swam the breast-stroke, lifting my head to breathe and make sure I kept my course. The lake was not perfectly round—it was a cinched oval, a giant peanut, and I swam a line that split it lengthwise. A shed, some part of the old quarry compound, came into view. A white house. I fixed my sight on it. The water splashed up into my ears. Halfway across, a bluegill leapt into the air and flopped its green-black body against the surface of the water.

When I got to the other side, I felt like I had crossed an ocean and was now climbing onto the shore of some other, weird land. I looked at the white house for a while, too scared to try to go inside. I found a zagging path behind it that let me back up the slope without having to crawl any farther.

A priest, especially a parish priest, is bound to be asked the same question over and over again his whole life.

Why did you decide to become a priest? When did you hear "the Calling"?

"The Calling," for most, is a myth. Ours is a long process of discernment. Boring conversations, strange elations, slow epiphanies. Dark nights, solitary funks. The proddings of meddling priests eager for new blood. But, still, some of us, if we're being honest with ourselves, can trace it back to some beginning, some faint stirring, and in this regard, I'm afraid I'm something of a cliché.

I came back to my dark neighborhood. Later, I found out there'd been a power outage, but at the time I felt that a blanket of darkness had been pulled over things. Or a blanket of false light had been stripped away, and now I could see the world for what it was. The sleepy cars, houses, and trees were all carved out of the same black block. I was carved out of it, too. Of course, I had no words for this. I just stood there, naked in the dark. And then I ran back inside and put my clothes on.

27

The next morning, I decided to take a long walk. To figure out if I was going to stay with Brian and Clara or keep on driving around and living out of my car. I promised myself I wouldn't come back until I'd made up my mind. Once Brian had left for work and Clara had gone out to her studio, I put on my only nonrancid T-shirt, stuck Paul's letter in my jacket pocket, picked a direction, and walked.

After the tent and the car, something about sleeping in a real bed had made my back feel even more tight and knotted, as if, like a stray dog taken in to a loving home, it took its newfound comfort as permission to act out. It was a bag of salt, grinding against itself whenever I moved.

My legs were sore, too, from the hike, but after a couple miles I broke through the strain and felt fine. I walked by a hospital, a community college, a woman sitting on a microwave and tweezing the final nub of a joint with a large pair of scissors.

Before long, I found myself walking across a short bridge along a busy road. I looked down over the rail, and suddenly the ground was a good eighty feet below me. I saw the tops of people's heads as they walked around. Thick, tall trees reached all the way up past the bridge, which helped camouflage the drop.

The air wafting up from the crevasse was piney and therapeutic. The clouds looked like scrambled eggs. I knew I could be happy here. But happiness was about as unappealing as the mayonnaise-white Heaven all the evangelicals advertise. Paul was right. I was a flagellant. I wanted my knees to pop. I wanted to wake up tired, with my back as stiff as Joan of Arc's pole. I needed to keep Paul as a cilice around my heart. I knew he'd forgive me, and probably had done so already, but that wasn't really the point. I didn't want forgiveness and the forgetting that comes with it. I wanted endless penance.

I found my way to the trail that led through the park. Ravenna Park was what it was called, a sign told me, because the whole thing was a giant ravine.

There were ferns the size of ceiling fans. Giant logs, thick as minivans, lay off to the sides of the path. The light mist, along with the ferns, moss, and logs, gave me the feeling I'd fallen into a primordial forest. Something from the movie *Jurassic Park*, maybe.

I found a bench and sat down. After a while, an old man walked over.

"Mind if I join you?" He was at least five years older than me. His nose had the same white hairs that I'd picked off of mine, except his were almost an inch long and leaned over the tip of his nose like pale vines spilling out of a flowerpot.

"Great day for a walk, huh? It's always a few degrees

cooler down here. It's its own little world. Thought I might do some reading."

He flashed the cover of the book in his hand. All I saw was the silhouette of what appeared to be an old-time gumshoe, a shadow of fedora and overcoat.

But instead of reading, he kept talking.

"If you don't mind me asking, when did you serve? I'm not a veteran myself," the man admitted. "I'm a doctor. I'm retired. But I can almost always tell when someone's been in the armed forces. It's just a look. I think it goes for nurses, too. There's—no offense—just a tiredness behind the face. A dead giveaway. I have a sense of these things."

"Vietnam," I lied.

"I figured it had to be. Well, thank you for your service."

I wiped my face on my sleeve.

"Oh no. It's okay. I'm sorry I brought it up. I'm sure you lost some good friends back there."

He handed me a red handkerchief from his pocket.

"No, it's okay."

"I mean, you get to our age and you have to ask yourself what you've got to show for things. I was an eye doctor. I helped people see. Sure, it was my job, but I did a good job at my job. I feel pretty good about that. I could have done more, maybe been a surgeon or volunteered more, but in my little way I did some useful things. You can say you gave something better than that, something truly substantial."

"I think I just need a minute. I'm sorry."

"I completely understand," he said. "I'm going to read. I'll be right here if you need anything."

"Thanks."

The anchorites of the Middle Ages had themselves built into churches. A room would be prepared, they'd step in, and then, after a sealing ceremony, they'd live out the rest of their lives as a fixture. Of course, they had a few sizable holes. And most were wealthy and had a servant to bring them food and books. This practice was especially popular among women, the most famous being Julian of Norwich, whose name, in keeping with the tradition among anchoresses, comes from the church in which she sealed herself. These women were granted special powers. People left contracts and wills in their care. Pilgrims came to their windows or peepholes, seeking advice, as Margery Kempe famously did with Julian.

I am an anchoress, too. I've sealed myself in the Church. I let it swallow me whole. I took a solemn vow. I pledged my allegiance to the flag. But what happens when it shows no loyalty to you? What happens when it spits you out?

I should have been there for Paul when I learned what Bruno did to him. I should have understood what had happened much sooner than that. I should have celebrated his wedding. I should have quit when I learned of the Brunos and all the ways the Church had covered them up. I should have urged my parish to follow the example of the nurse and continue our work in Haiti. I should have called on them in other ways, too. I should have lit a fire under them, steered them toward justice, holiness, and truth. We should have been stewards of our dying planet. We should have fed the hungry, visited those in prison, healed the sick. We should have taken better care of one another.

☙

The man left. I stayed on the bench, staring at the ferns and lanky trees. I put my hands in my pockets and felt something strange in one of them, a whorled cone. It was the goat's horn, from Paul's cemetery. I ran my fingers along the little ridges.

I blew into it, but of course it made no sound. The walls of my life didn't come tumbling down.

As I got up, I heard a rustling in the brush behind me. I turned around, and a bush began to shake. Something was in it.

I waited to see what it was.

Acknowledgments

Thank you to my agent, Chris Clemans, whose deep insight transformed the manuscript, and whose savvy counsel kept its heart intact. And to my brilliant editor Anna Kaufman—your vision and energy throughout this process were simply astounding. If I were pope, I'd canonize you both. To Terry Zaroff-Evans, whose copyedits had the intensity and salubrious effect of a Swedish sauna. To Kevin Bourke, Maria Carella, Rose Cronin-Jackman, Julianne Clancy, Chris Jerome, and Tyler Comrie for all your amazing work, and to Kathy Hourigan for championing this book.

To everyone who read this manuscript in some form or another: Courtney Sender, Tim Delong, Monika Woods, Anna Sheaffer, Steven Cook, Chris McCormick, Andrew Martin, Chigozie Obioma, and Brit Bennett.

To my mentors and teachers at Kansas State, the University of Michigan, and HDS, especially Dan Hoyt, Peter Ho Davies, Sugi Ganeshananthan, Nick Delbanco, Elizabeth Dodd, Katherine Karlin, and Lisa Tatonetti. Matt Potts, Stephanie Paulsell, and Father John Kiefer gave me a trove of insights and anecdotes peppered throughout the book.

To my Memphis family: Karyna McGlynn, Brent Nobles, Marcus Wicker, Emily Skaja, and Caki Wilkinson.

Acknowledgments

I'm forever grateful for the friendship of some of my oldest collaborators: John Goddard, Kristin Henry, and Ryan Manes.

I'd be nothing without the love and support of my mother and father, Peg and Jeff Hornsby. And thank you to the rest of my family, especially Michael and Brigid, Kate Nolan, Dan Nolan, Grandma Rose, and Mary and Bob Bolin.

And finally, to Alice, my love.

A NOTE ON THE TYPE

This book was set in a version of Monotype Baskerville, the antecedent of which was a typeface designed by John Baskerville (1706–1775). Baskerville's types, distinctive and elegant in design, are a forerunner of what we know today as the "modern" group of typefaces.

Typeset by Digital Composition, Berryville, Virginia
Printed and bound by Friesens, Altona, Manitoba
Designed by Maria Carella

A NOTE ABOUT THE AUTHOR

Daniel Hornsby was born in Muncie, Indiana. He holds an M.F.A. in fiction from the University of Michigan, and an M.T.S. from Harvard Divinity School. His stories and essays have appeared in the *Los Angeles Review of Books, Electric Literature, The Missouri Review,* and *Joyland.* He lives in Memphis, Tennessee.